D1254079

AVENGERS K #1
THE ADVENT OF ULTRON

JIM ZUB
SCRIPT

WOO BIN CHOI with **JAE SUNG LEE**
PENCILS

MIN JU LEE
INKS

JAE WOONG LEE
COLORS

VC's CORY PETIT
LETTERS

WOO BIN CHOI WITH **JAE SUNG LEE, MIN JU LEE** & **JAE WOONG LEE**
COVER ART

AVENGERS VS. ULTRON is adapted from AVENGERS ORIGINS: SCARLET WITCH & QUICKSILVER #1,
AVENGERS ORIGINS: ANT-MAN & THE WASP #1, and AVENGERS (1963) #57.
Adaptations written by SI YEON PARK and translated by JI EUN PARK

AVENGERS created by STAN LEE and JACK KIRBY

Original comics written by SEAN McKEEVER, ROBERTO AGUIRRE-SACASA, and ROY THOMAS;
and illustrated by MIRCO PIERFEDERICI, STEPHANIE HANS, and JOHN BUSCEMA

Editor SARAH BRUNSTAD
Manager, Licensed Publishing JEFF REINGOLD
VP, Brand Management & Development, Asia C.B. CEBULSKI
VP, Production & Special Projects JEFF YOUNGQUIST
SVP Print, Sales & Marketing DAVID GABRIEL
Associate Manager, Digital Assets JOE HOCHSTEIN
Associate Managing Editor ALEX STARBUCK
Senior Editor, Special Projects JENNIFER GRÜNWALD
Editor, Special Projects MARK D. BEAZLEY
Book Designer ADAM DEL RE

Editor In Chief AXEL ALONSO
Chief Creative Officer JOE QUESADA
President DAN BUCKLEY
Executive Producer ALAN FINE

ABDO
Spotlight

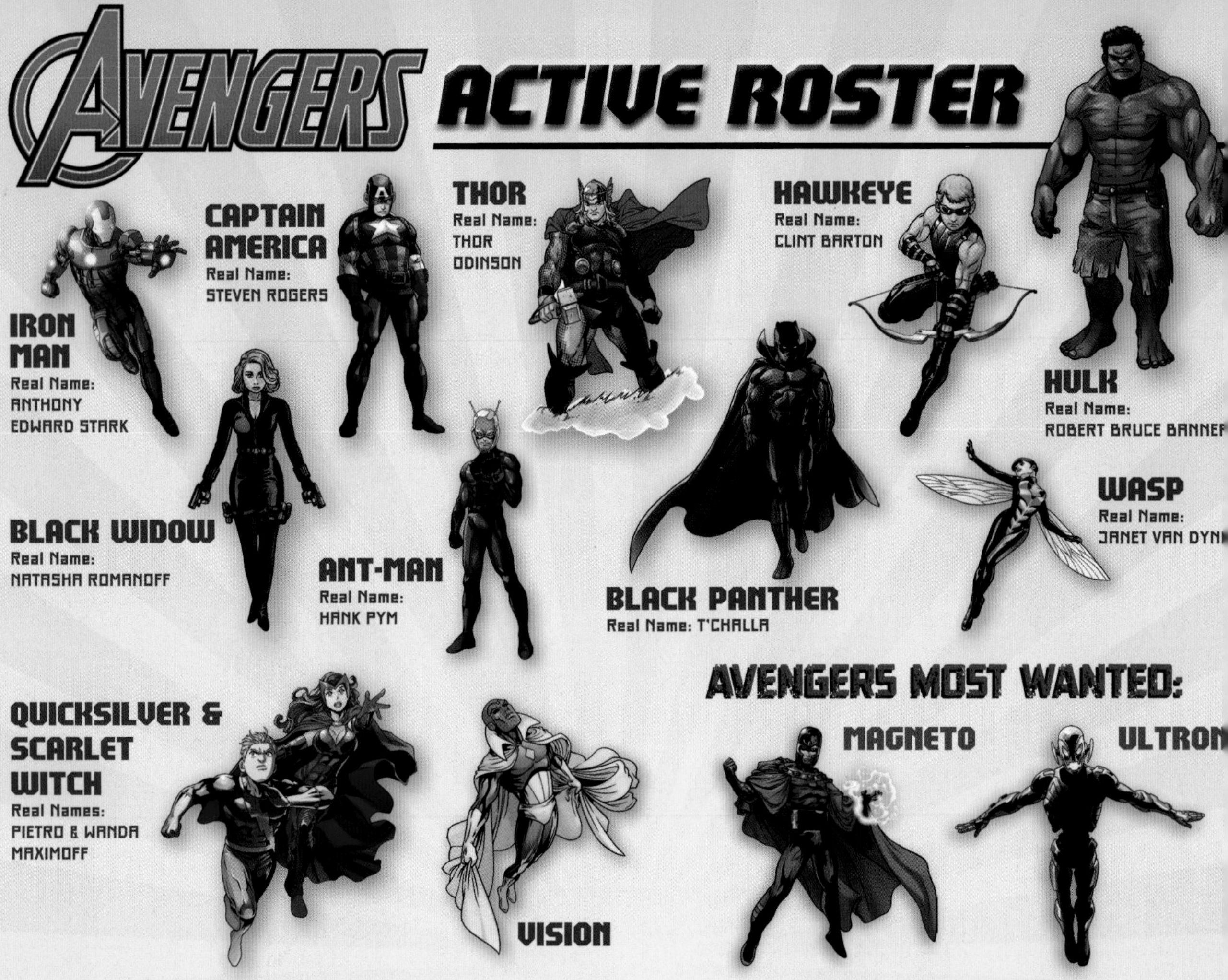

AVENGERS
ACTIVE ROSTER
IRON MAN
Real Name:
ANTHONY EDWARD STARK
CAPTAIN AMERICA
Real Name:
STEVEN ROGERS
THOR
Real Name:
THOR ODINSON
HAWKEYE
Real Name:
CLINT BARTON
HULK
Real Name:
ROBERT BRUCE BANNE
BLACK WIDOW
Real Name:
NATASHA ROMANOFF
ANT-MAN
Real Name:
HANK PYM
BLACK PANTHER
Real Name: T'CHALLA
WASP
Real Name:
JANET VAN DYN
QUICKSILVER & SCARLET WITCH
Real Names:
PIETRO & WANDA MAXIMOFF
VISION
AVENGERS MOST WANTED:
MAGNETO
ULTRON

ABDOPUBLISHING.COM

Reinforced library bound edition published in 2018 by Spotlight, a division of ABDO, PO Box 398166, Minneapolis, Minnesota 55439. Spotlight produces high-quality reinforced library bound editions for schools and libraries. Published by agreement with Marvel Characters, Inc.
Printed in the United States of America, North Mankato, Minnesota.
042017 092017

marvelkids.com

PUBLISHER'S CATALOGING IN PUBLICATION DATA

Names: Zub, Jim, author. | Choi, Woo Bin ; Lee, Jae Sung ; Lee, Min Ju ; Lee, Jae Woong, illustrators.
Title: The advent of Ultron / writer: Jim Zub ; art: Woo Bin Choi ; Jae Sung Lee ; Min Ju Lee ; Jae Woong Lee.
Description: Reinforced library bound edition. | Minneapolis, Minnesota : Spotlight, 2018. | Series: Avengers K Set 2
Summary: Learn about the beginnings of your favorite Avengers, including Quicksilver and the Scarlet Witch's time with Magneto, how Ant-Man and the Wasp became a team, and the Vision's struggle to understand where he came from.
Identifiers: LCCN 2016961923 | ISBN 9781532140013 (v.1 ; lib. bdg.) | ISBN 9781532140020 (v.2 ; lib. bdg.) | ISBN 9781532140037 (v.3 ; lib. bdg.) | ISBN 9781532140044 (v.4 ; lib. bdg.) | ISBN 9781532140051 (v.5 ; lib. bdg.) | ISBN 9781532140068 (v.6 ; lib. bdg.)
Subjects: LCSH: Avengers (Fictitious characters)--Juvenile fiction. | Adventure and adventurers--Juvenile fiction. | Comic books, strips, etc.--Juvenile fiction. | Graphic novels--Juvenile fiction.
Classification: DDC 741.5--dc23
LC record available at https://lccn.loc.gov/2016961923

ABDO
Spotlight

A Division of ABDO
abdopublishing.com

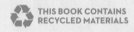

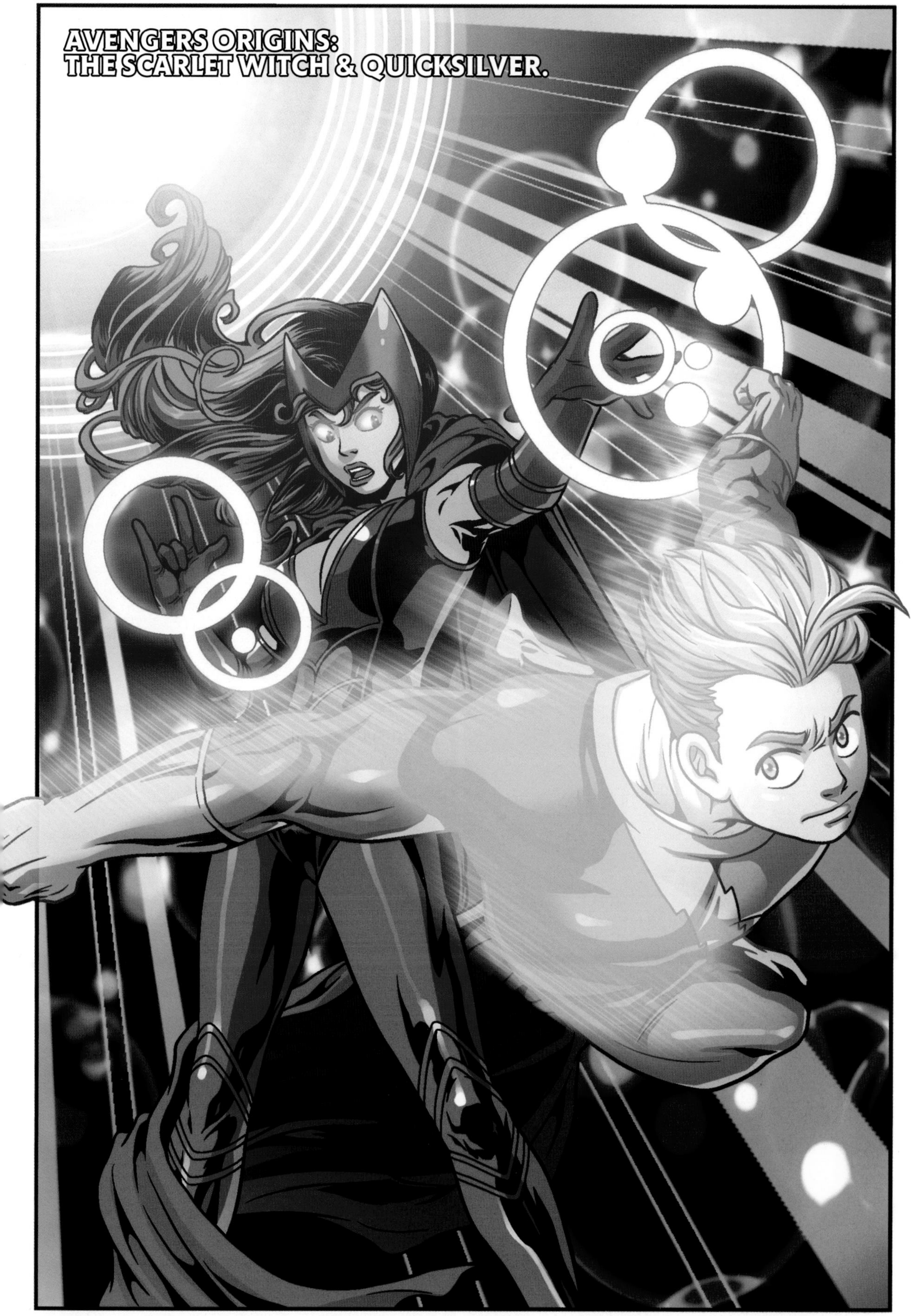
AVENGERS ORIGINS:
THE SCARLET WITCH & QUICKSILVER.

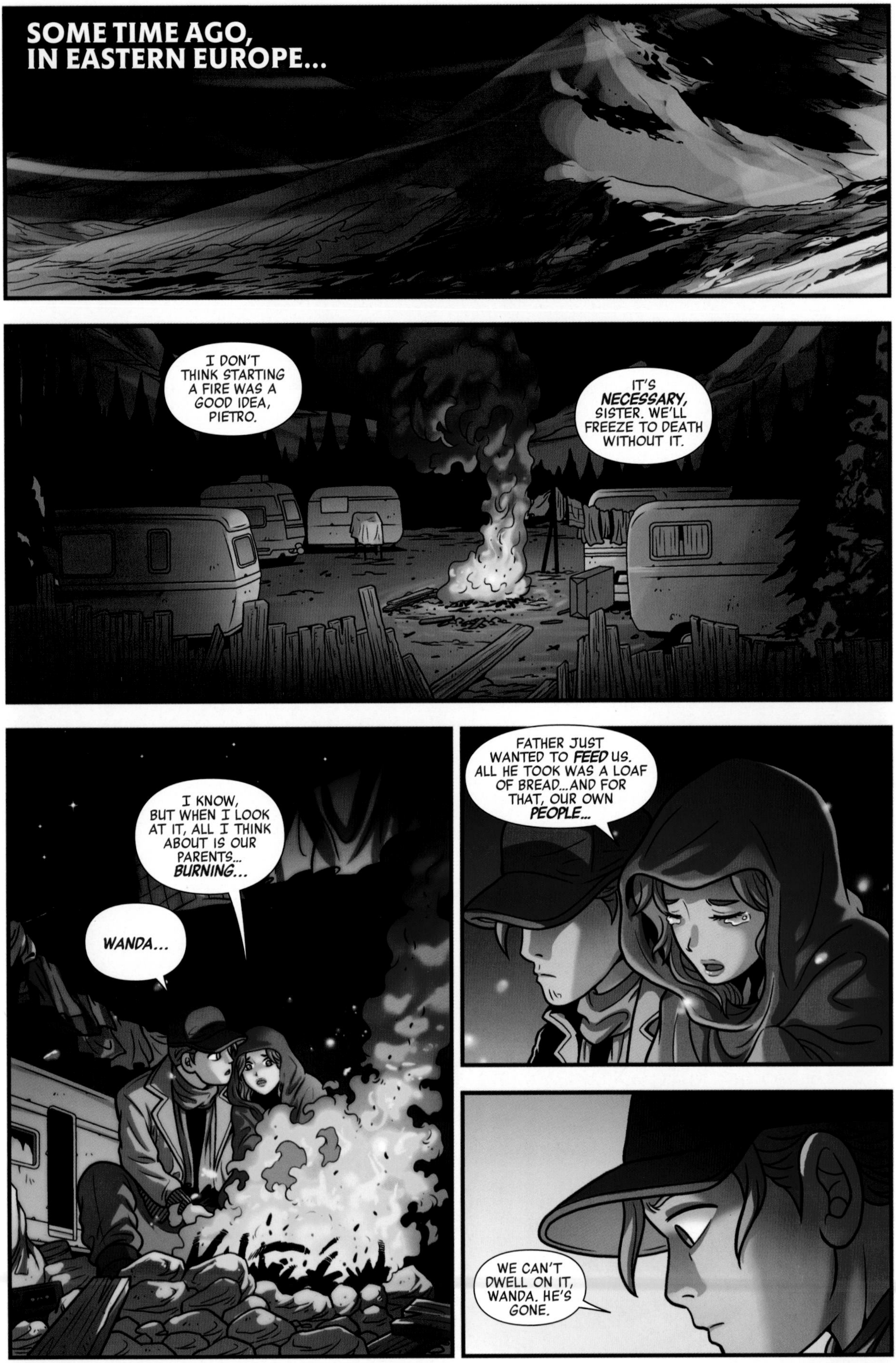
SOME TIME AGO, IN EASTERN EUROPE...
I DON'T THINK STARTING A FIRE WAS A GOOD IDEA, PIETRO.
IT'S NECESSARY, SISTER. WE'LL FREEZE TO DEATH WITHOUT IT.
I KNOW, BUT WHEN I LOOK AT IT, ALL I THINK ABOUT IS OUR PARENTS... BURNING...
WANDA...
FATHER JUST WANTED TO FEED US. ALL HE TOOK WAS A LOAF OF BREAD...AND FOR THAT, OUR OWN PEOPLE...
WE CAN'T DWELL ON IT, WANDA. HE'S GONE.

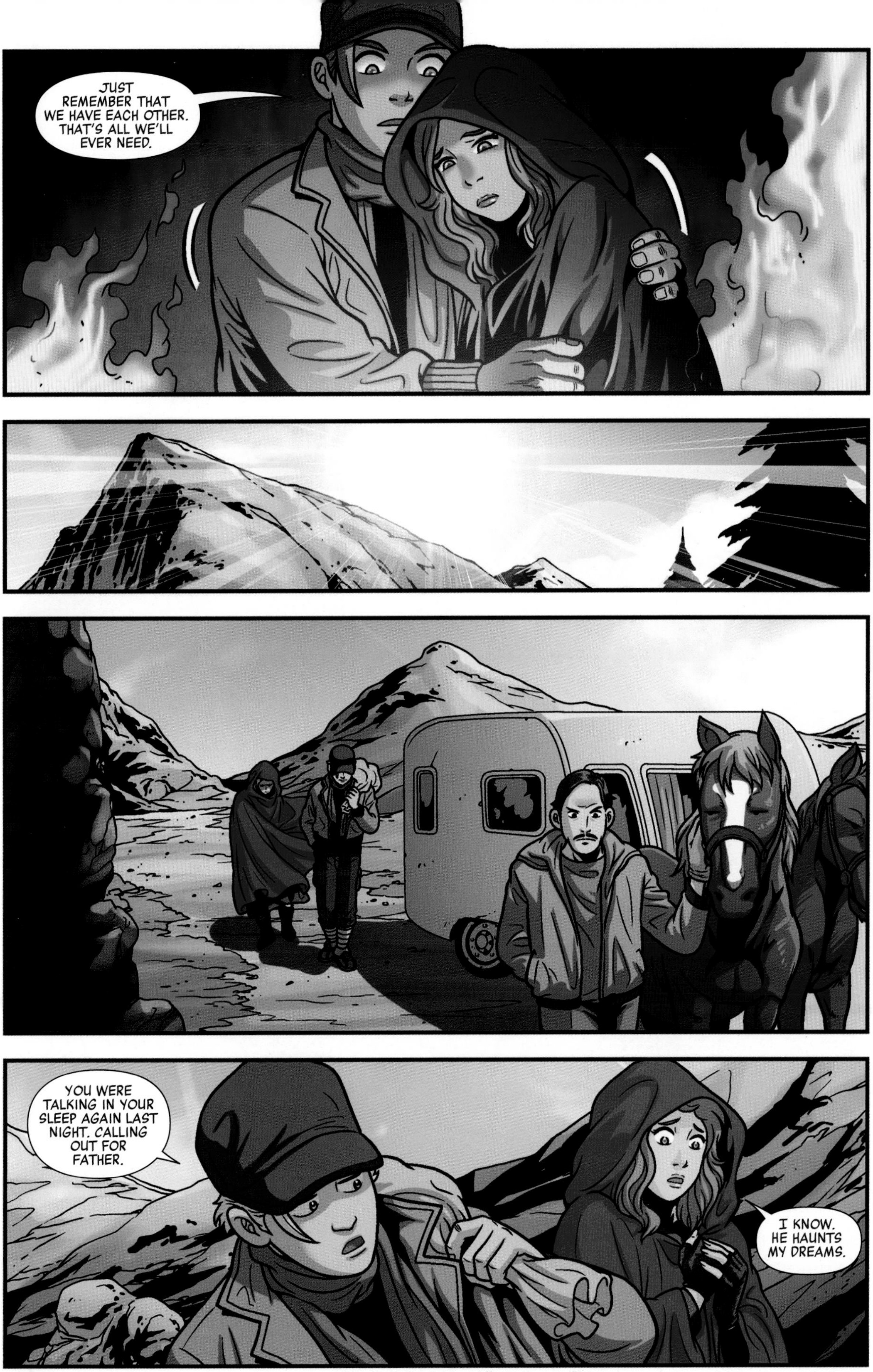
JUST REMEMBER THAT WE HAVE EACH OTHER. THAT'S ALL WE'LL EVER NEED.
YOU WERE TALKING IN YOUR SLEEP AGAIN LAST NIGHT. CALLING OUT FOR FATHER.
I KNOW. HE HAUNTS MY DREAMS.

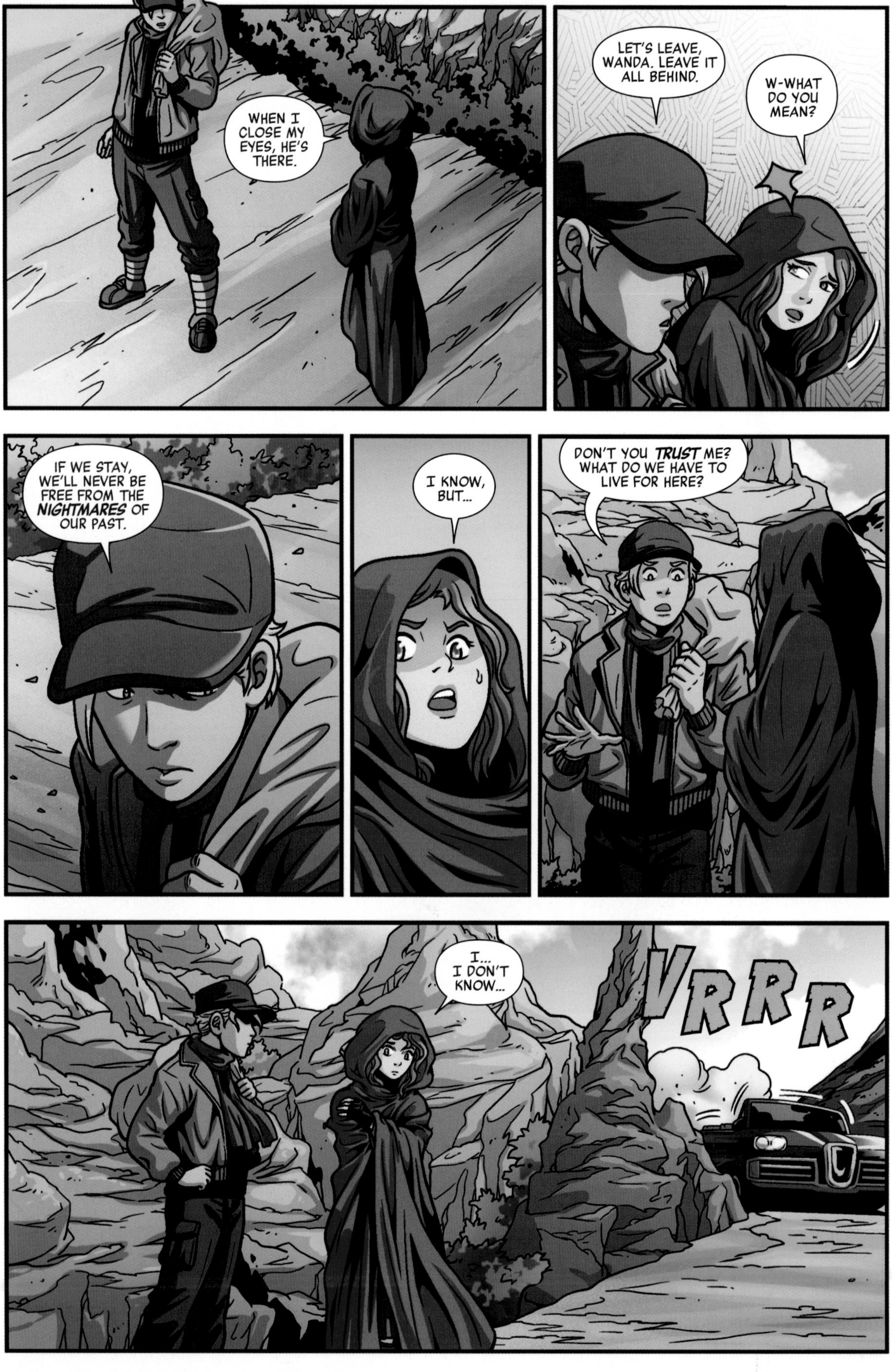
WHEN I CLOSE MY EYES, HE'S THERE.
LET'S LEAVE, WANDA. LEAVE IT ALL BEHIND.
W-WHAT DO YOU MEAN?
IF WE STAY, WE'LL NEVER BE FREE FROM THE NIGHTMARES OF OUR PAST.
I KNOW, BUT...
DON'T YOU TRUST ME? WHAT DO WE HAVE TO LIVE FOR HERE?
I... I DON'T KNOW...
VRRR

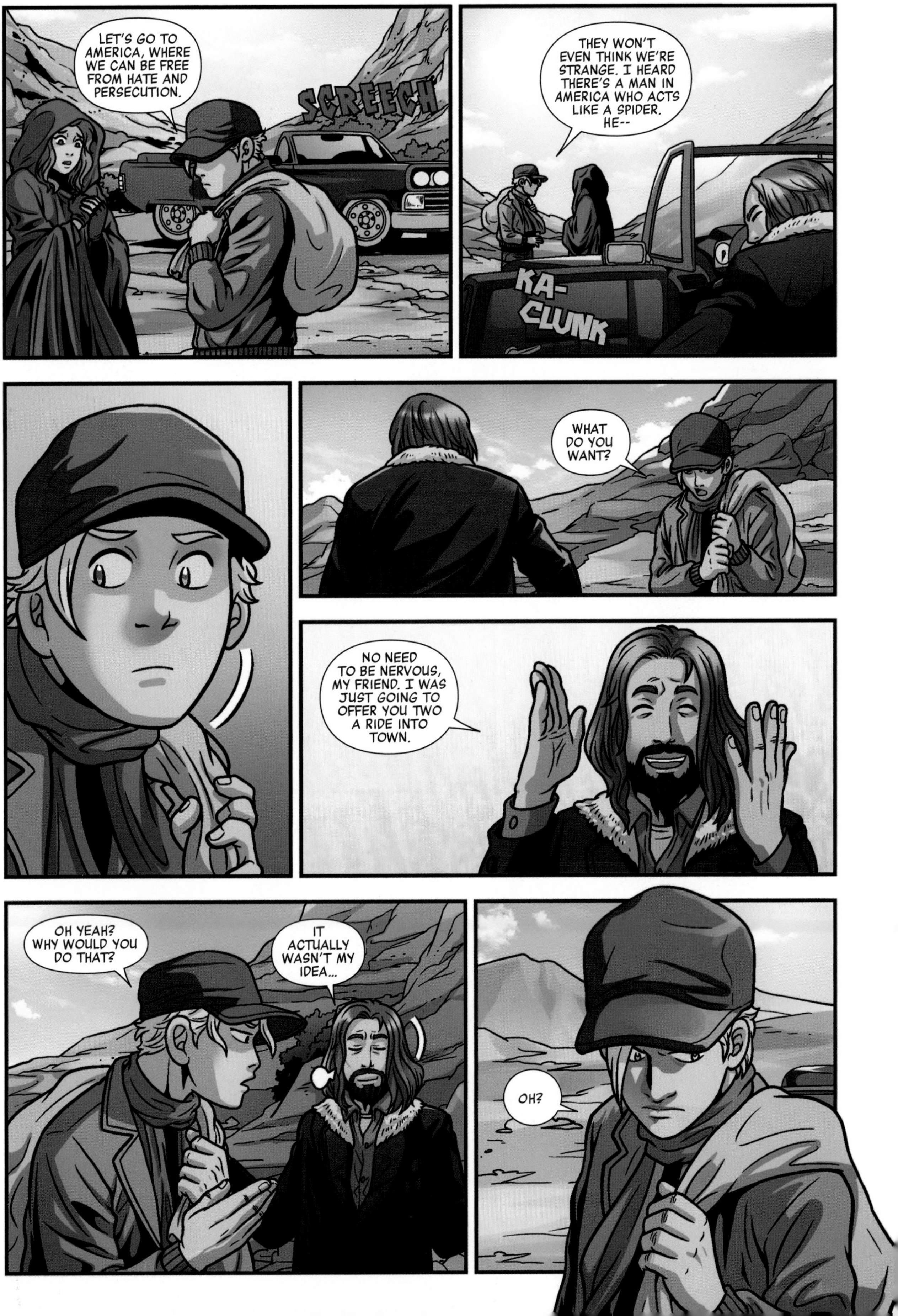
LET'S GO TO AMERICA, WHERE WE CAN BE FREE FROM HATE AND PERSECUTION.
SCREECH
THEY WON'T EVEN THINK WE'RE STRANGE. I HEARD THERE'S A MAN IN AMERICA WHO ACTS LIKE A SPIDER. HE--
KA-CLUNK
WHAT DO YOU WANT?
NO NEED TO BE NERVOUS, MY FRIEND. I WAS JUST GOING TO OFFER YOU TWO A RIDE INTO TOWN.
OH YEAH? WHY WOULD YOU DO THAT?
IT ACTUALLY WASN'T MY IDEA...
OH?

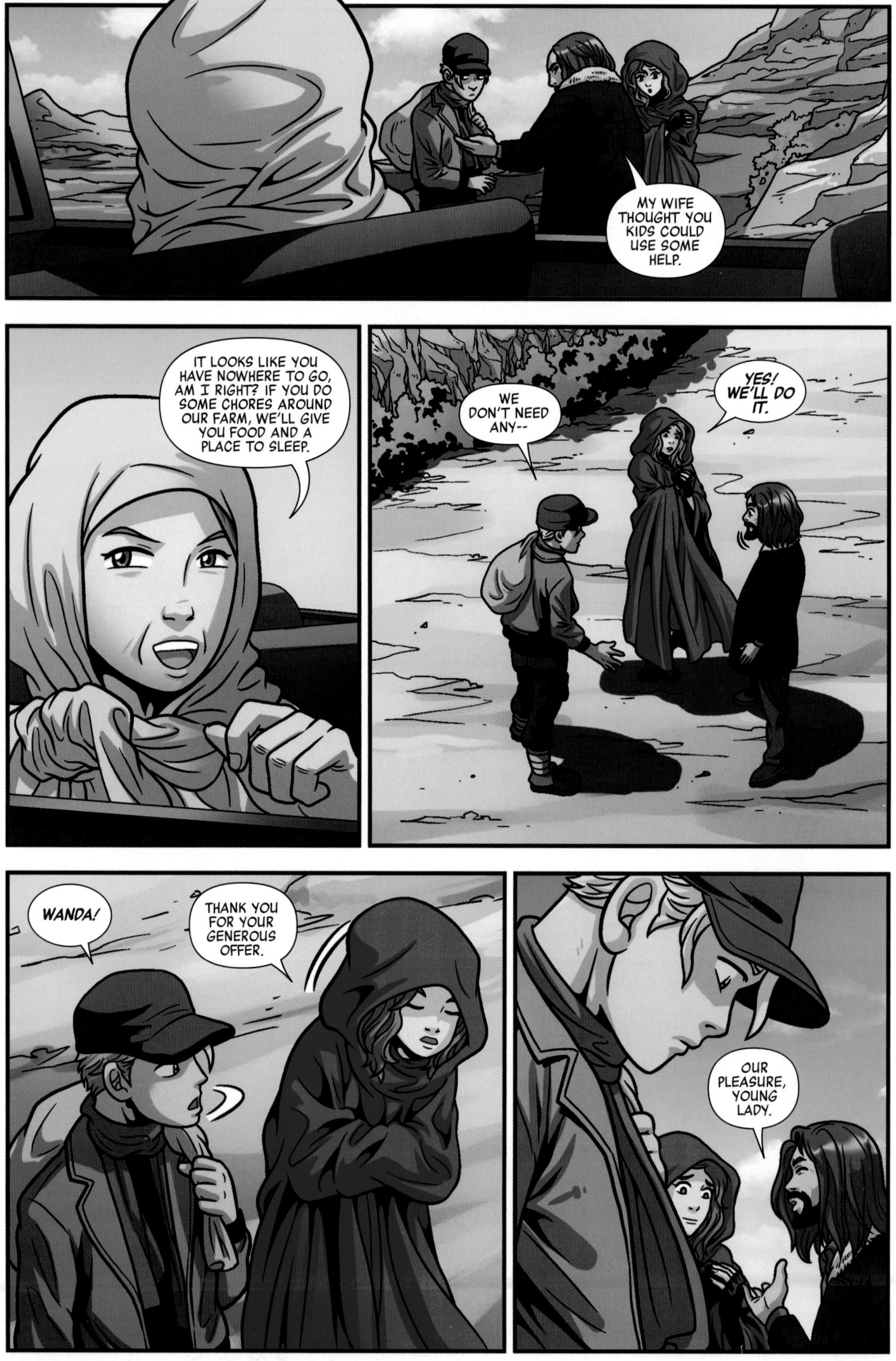
MY WIFE THOUGHT YOU KIDS COULD USE SOME HELP.
IT LOOKS LIKE YOU HAVE NOWHERE TO GO, AM I RIGHT? IF YOU DO SOME CHORES AROUND OUR FARM, WE'LL GIVE YOU FOOD AND A PLACE TO SLEEP.
WE DON'T NEED ANY--
YES! WE'LL DO IT.
WANDA!
THANK YOU FOR YOUR GENEROUS OFFER.
OUR PLEASURE, YOUNG LADY.

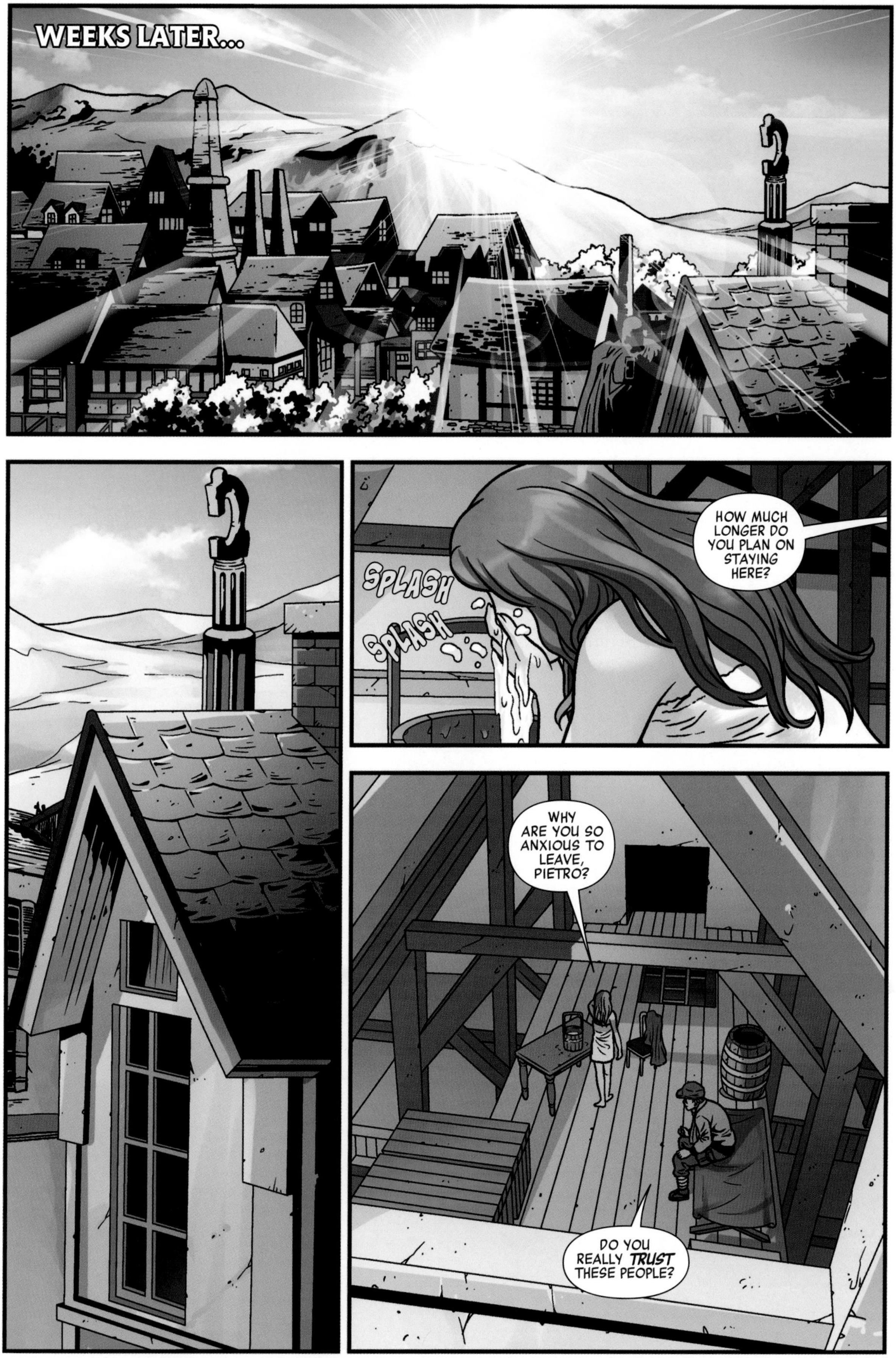
WEEKS LATER...
SPLASH
SPLASH
HOW MUCH LONGER DO YOU PLAN ON STAYING HERE?
WHY ARE YOU SO ANXIOUS TO LEAVE, PIETRO?
DO YOU REALLY TRUST THESE PEOPLE?

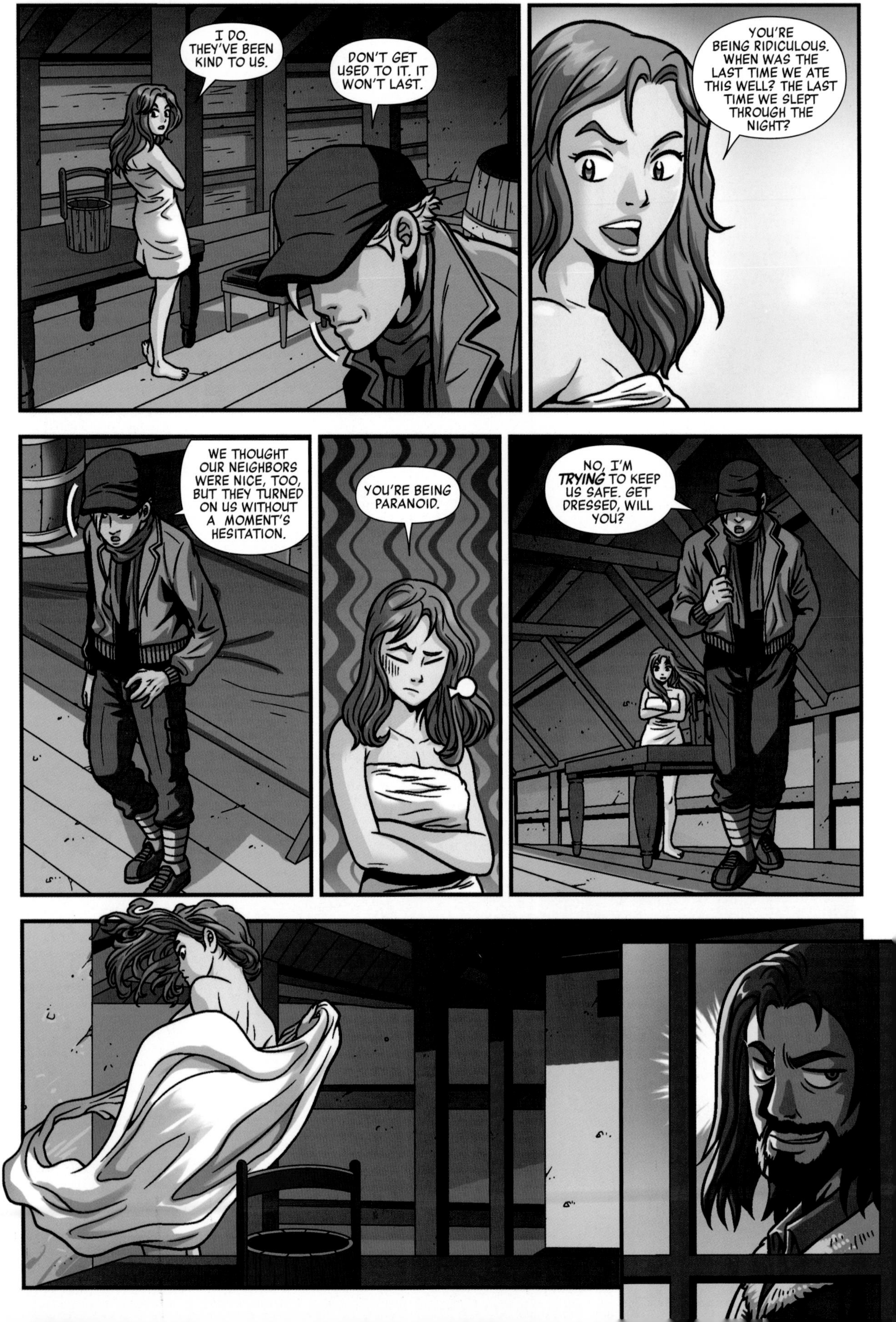
I DO. THEY'VE BEEN KIND TO US.
DON'T GET USED TO IT. IT WON'T LAST.
YOU'RE BEING RIDICULOUS. WHEN WAS THE LAST TIME WE ATE THIS WELL? THE LAST TIME WE SLEPT THROUGH THE NIGHT?
WE THOUGHT OUR NEIGHBORS WERE NICE, TOO, BUT THEY TURNED ON US WITHOUT A MOMENT'S HESITATION.
YOU'RE BEING PARANOID.
NO, I'M *TRYING* TO KEEP US SAFE. GET DRESSED, WILL YOU?

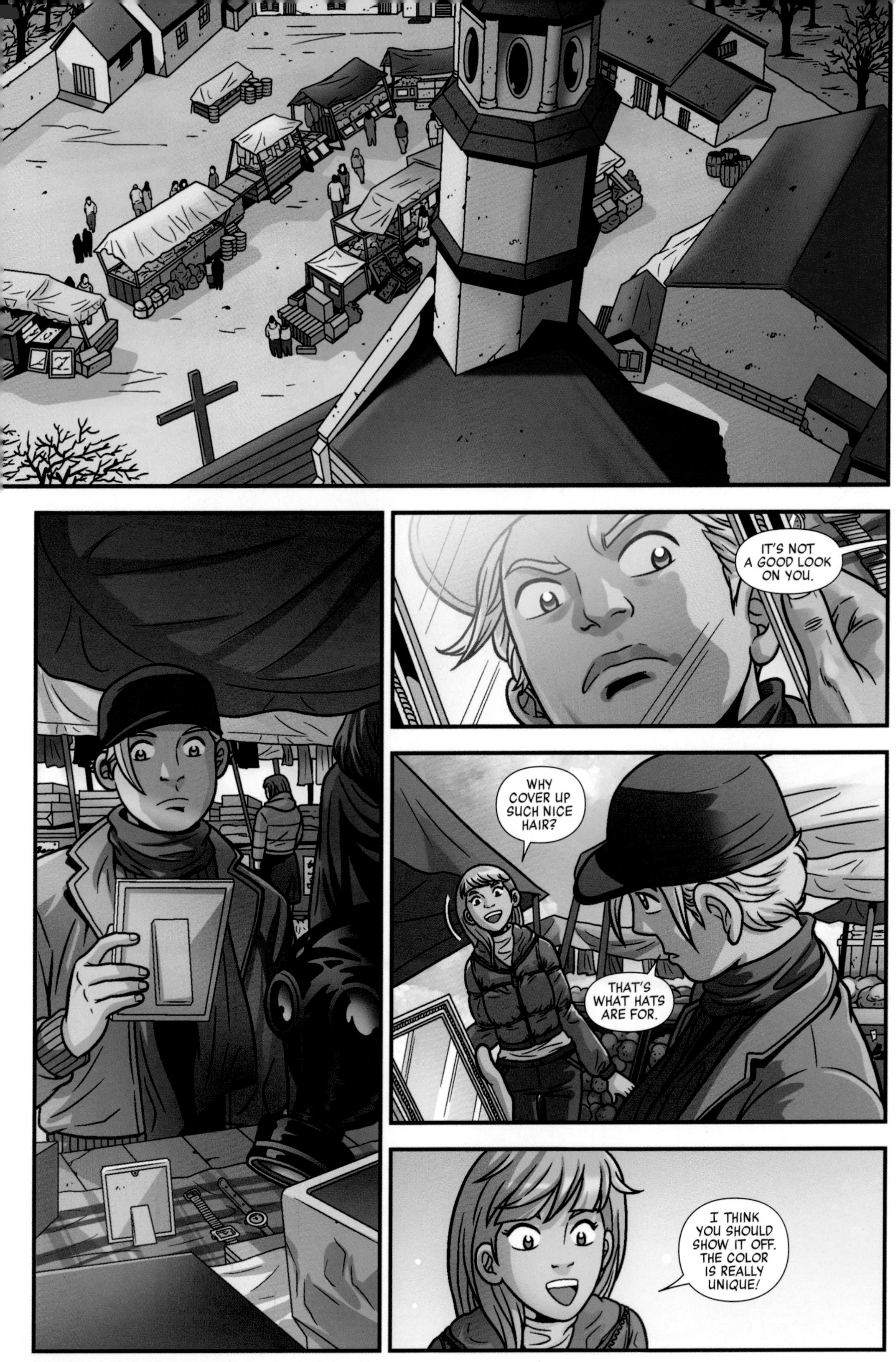
IT'S NOT A GOOD LOOK ON YOU.
WHY COVER UP SUCH NICE HAIR?
THAT'S WHAT HATS ARE FOR.
I THINK YOU SHOULD SHOW IT OFF. THE COLOR IS REALLY UNIQUE!

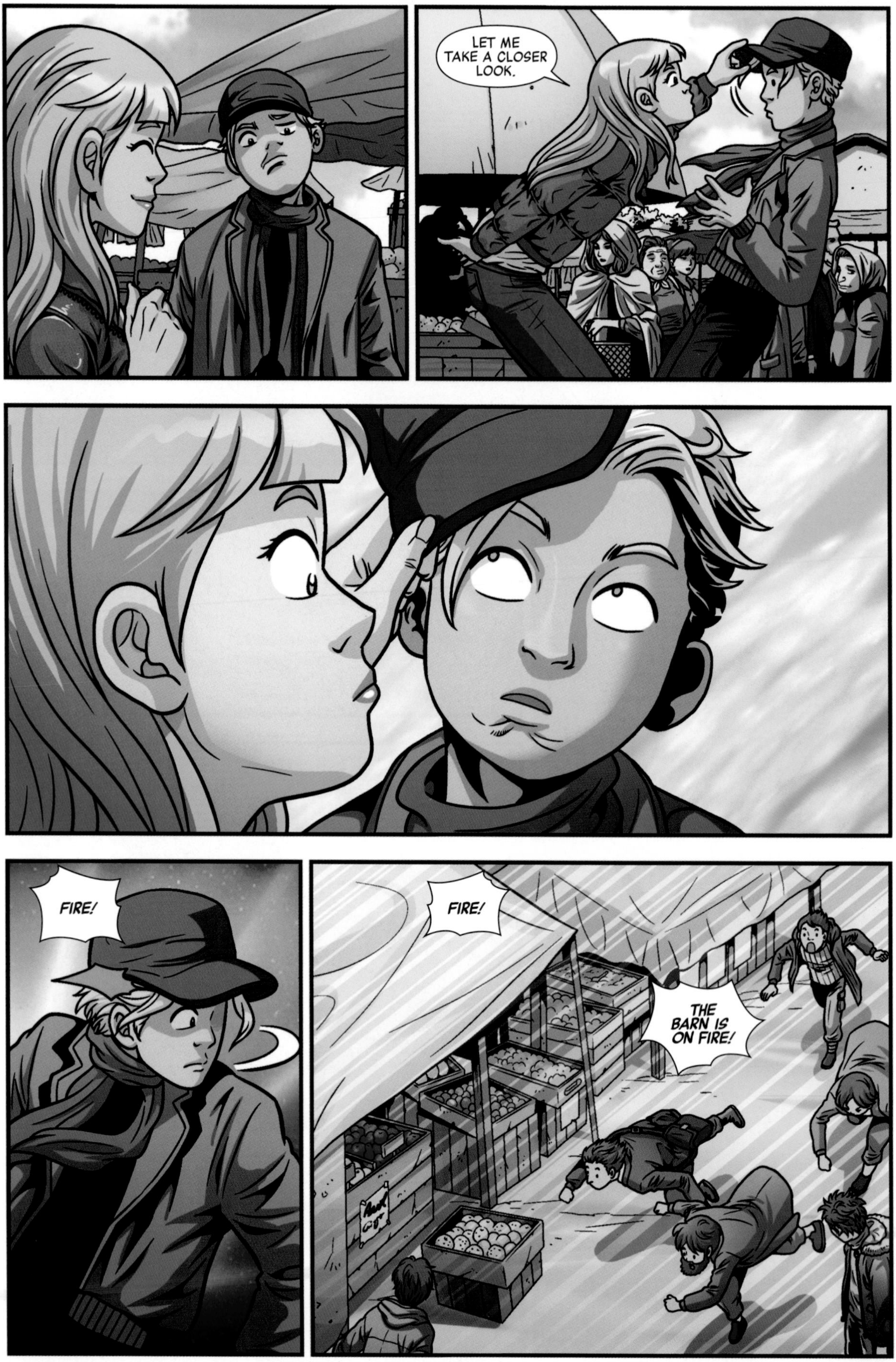
LET ME TAKE A CLOSER LOOK.
FIRE!
FIRE!
THE BARN IS ON FIRE!

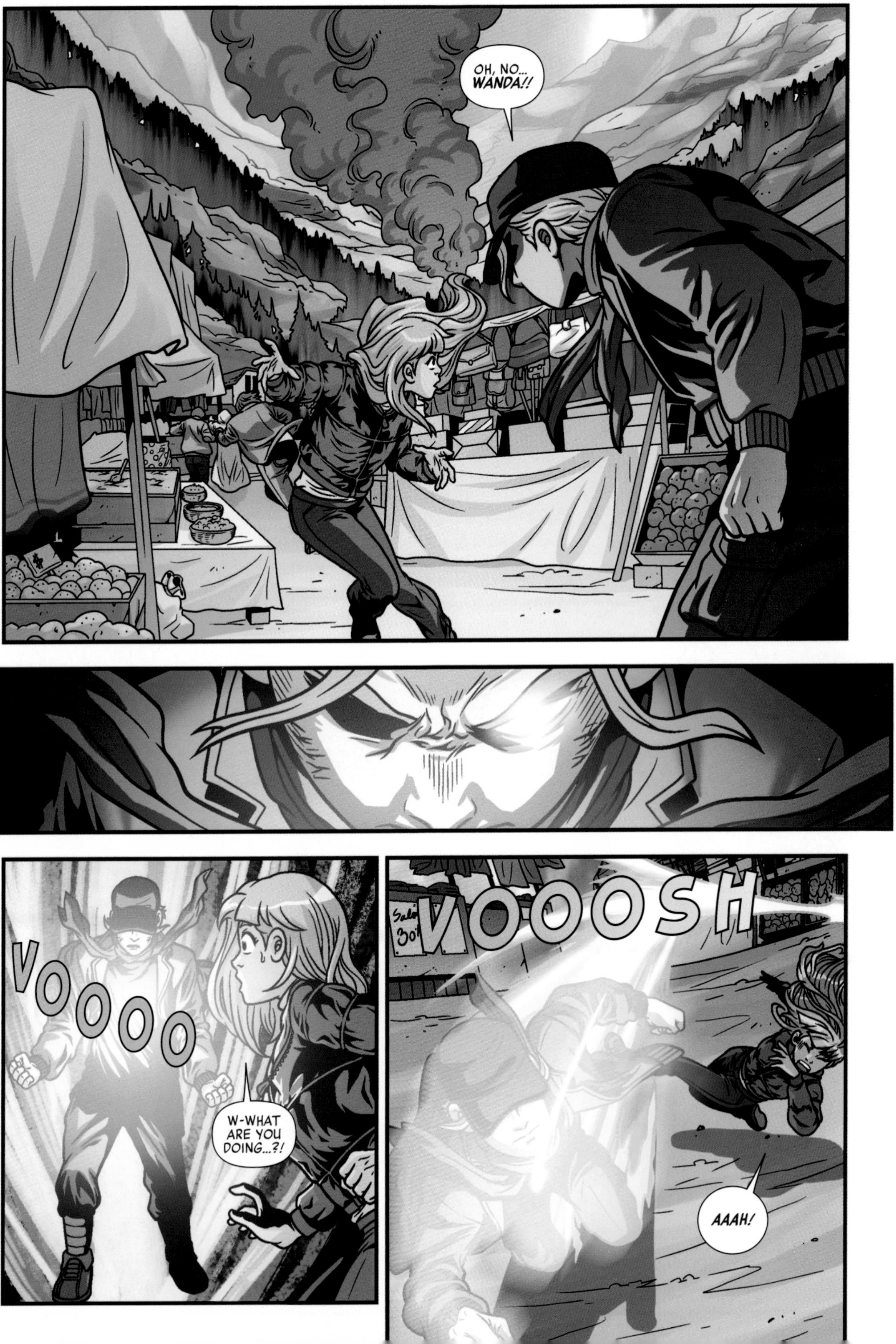
OH, NO... WANDA!!
VOOOO
W-WHAT ARE YOU DOING...?!
VOOOSH
AAAH!

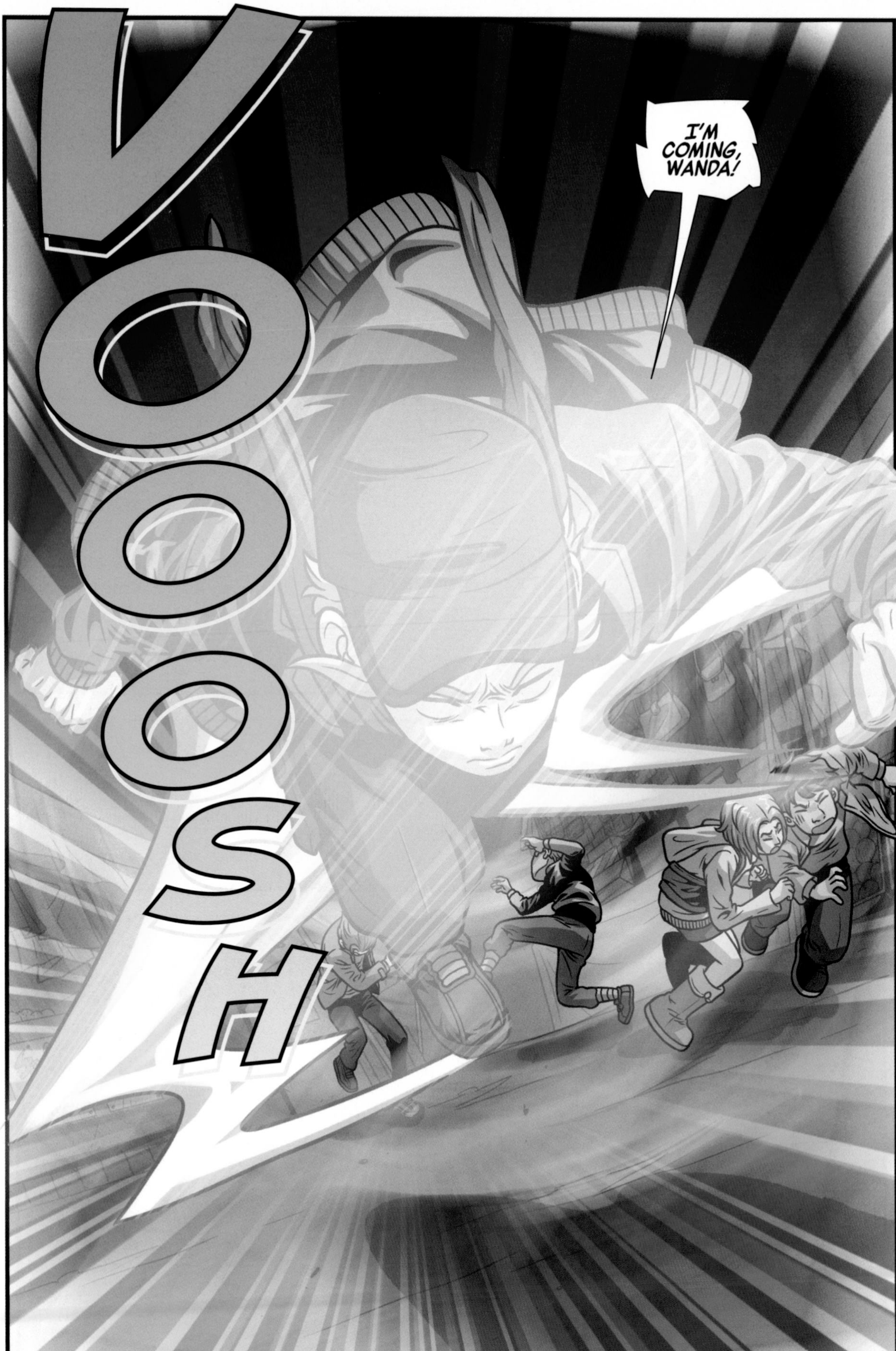
VOOOOSH
I'M COMING, WANDA!

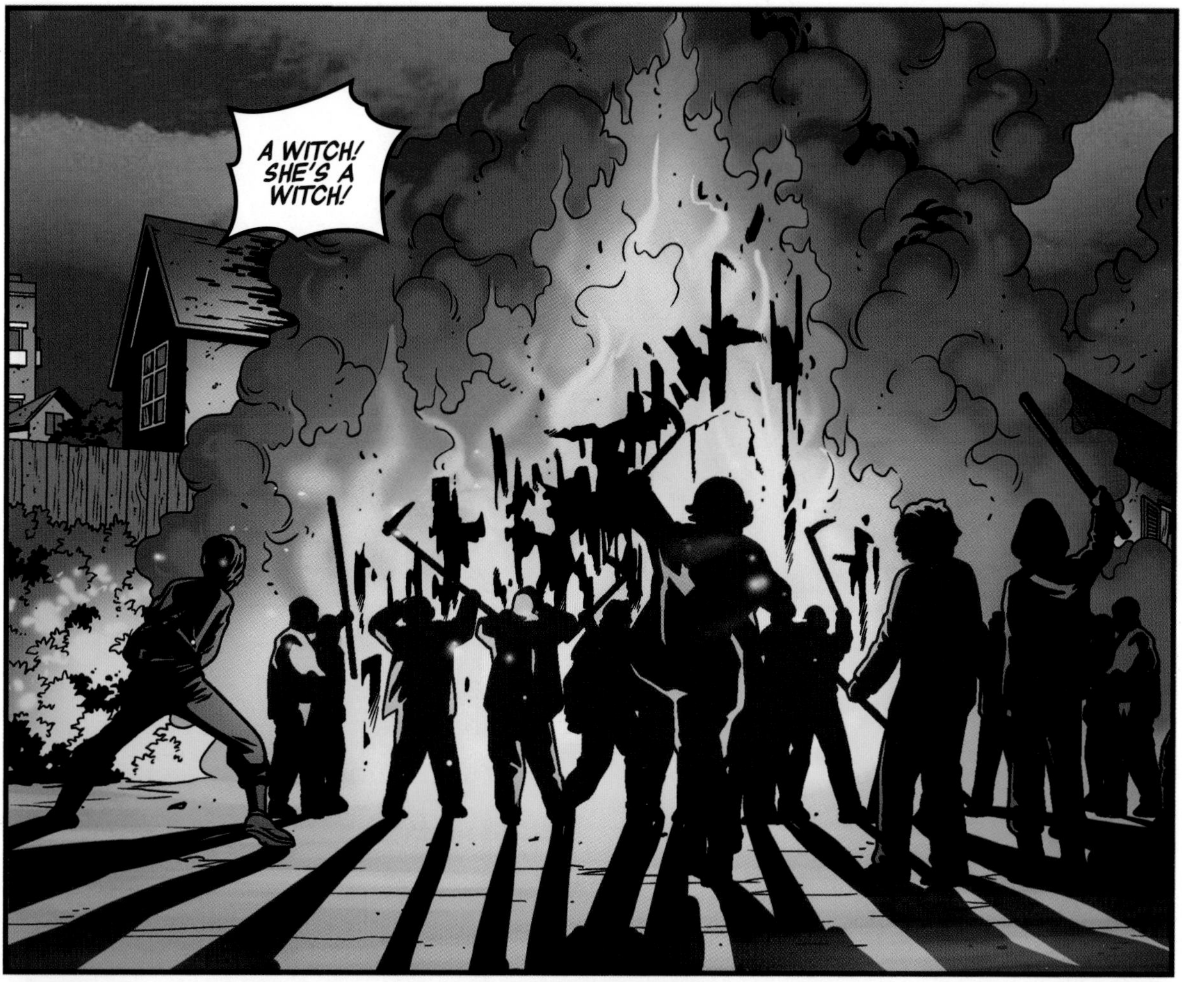
A WITCH! SHE'S A WITCH!

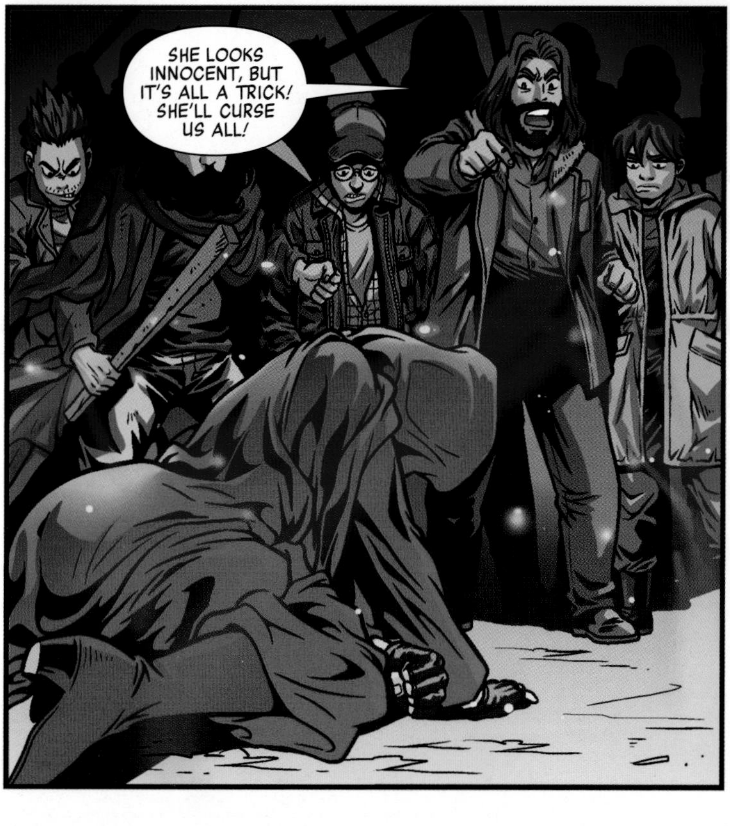
SHE LOOKS INNOCENT, BUT IT'S ALL A TRICK! SHE'LL CURSE US ALL!

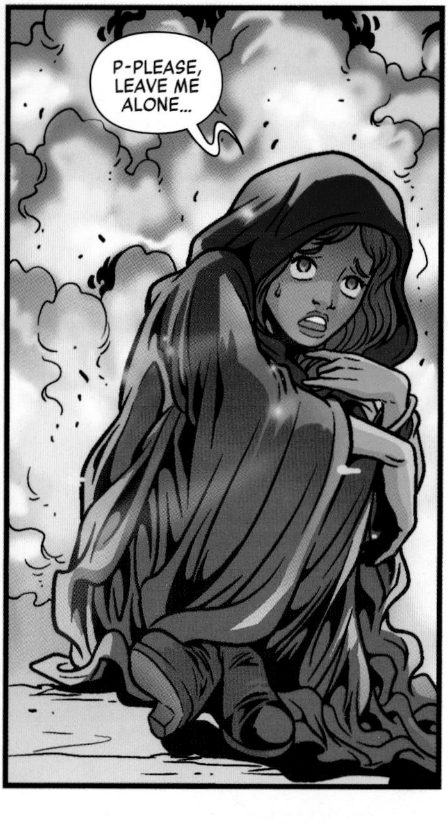
P-PLEASE, LEAVE ME ALONE...

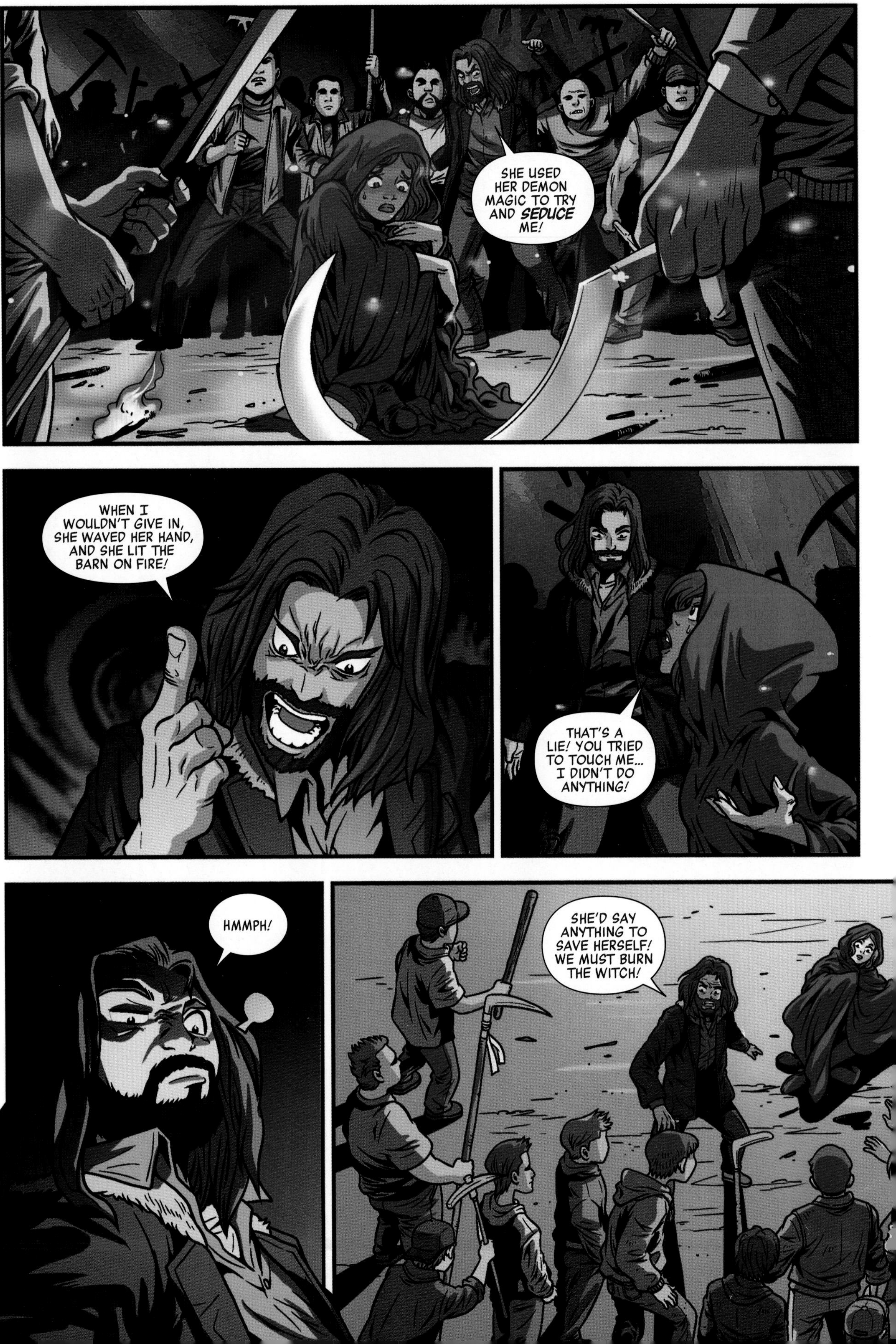
SHE USED HER DEMON MAGIC TO TRY AND **SEDUCE** ME!
WHEN I WOULDN'T GIVE IN, SHE WAVED HER HAND, AND SHE LIT THE BARN ON FIRE!
THAT'S A LIE! YOU TRIED TO TOUCH ME... I DIDN'T DO ANYTHING!
HMMPH!
SHE'D SAY ANYTHING TO SAVE HERSELF! WE MUST BURN THE WITCH!

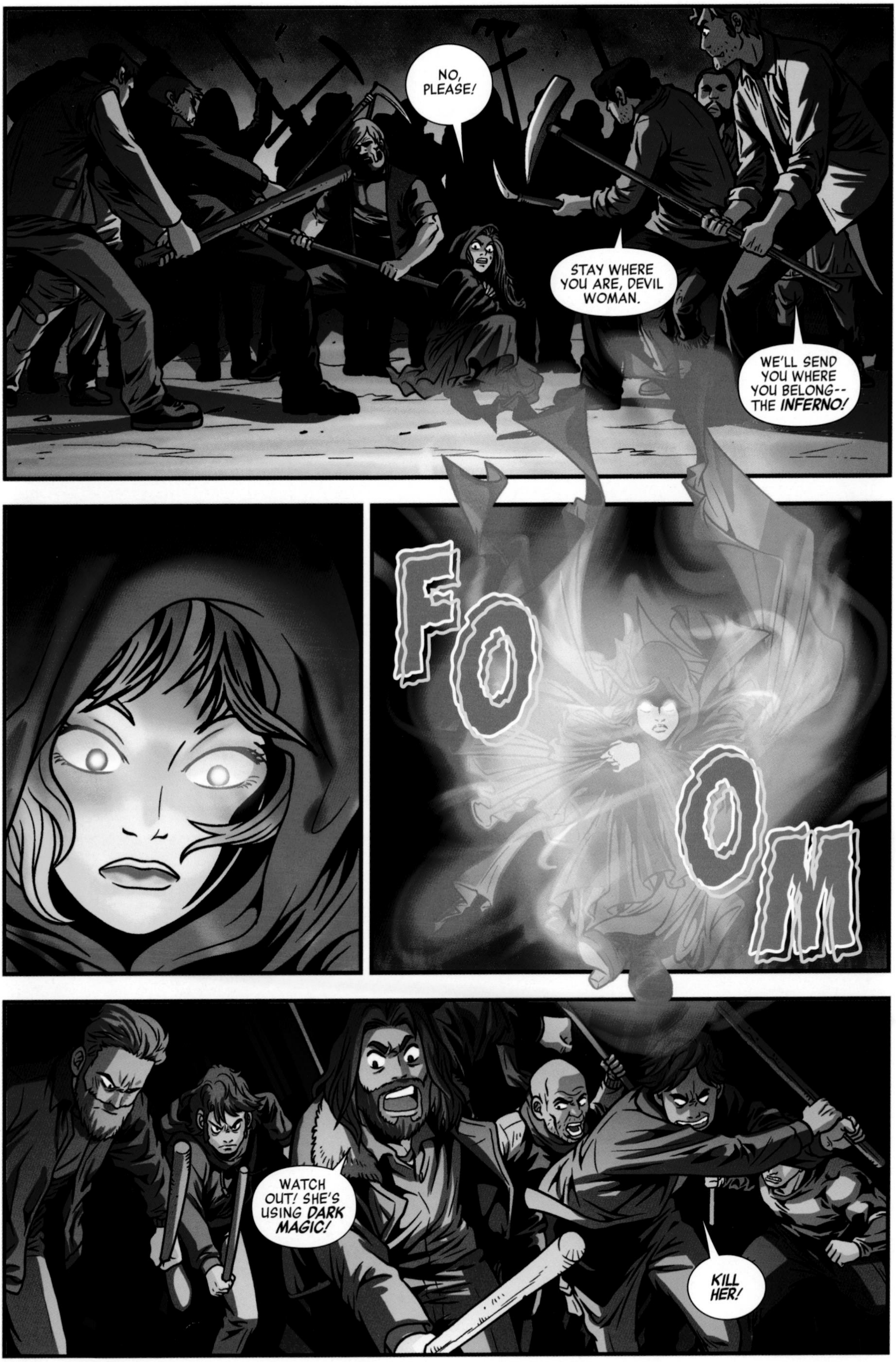
NO, PLEASE!
STAY WHERE YOU ARE, DEVIL WOMAN.
WE'LL SEND YOU WHERE YOU BELONG-- THE INFERNO!
FOOOM
WATCH OUT! SHE'S USING DARK MAGIC!
KILL HER!

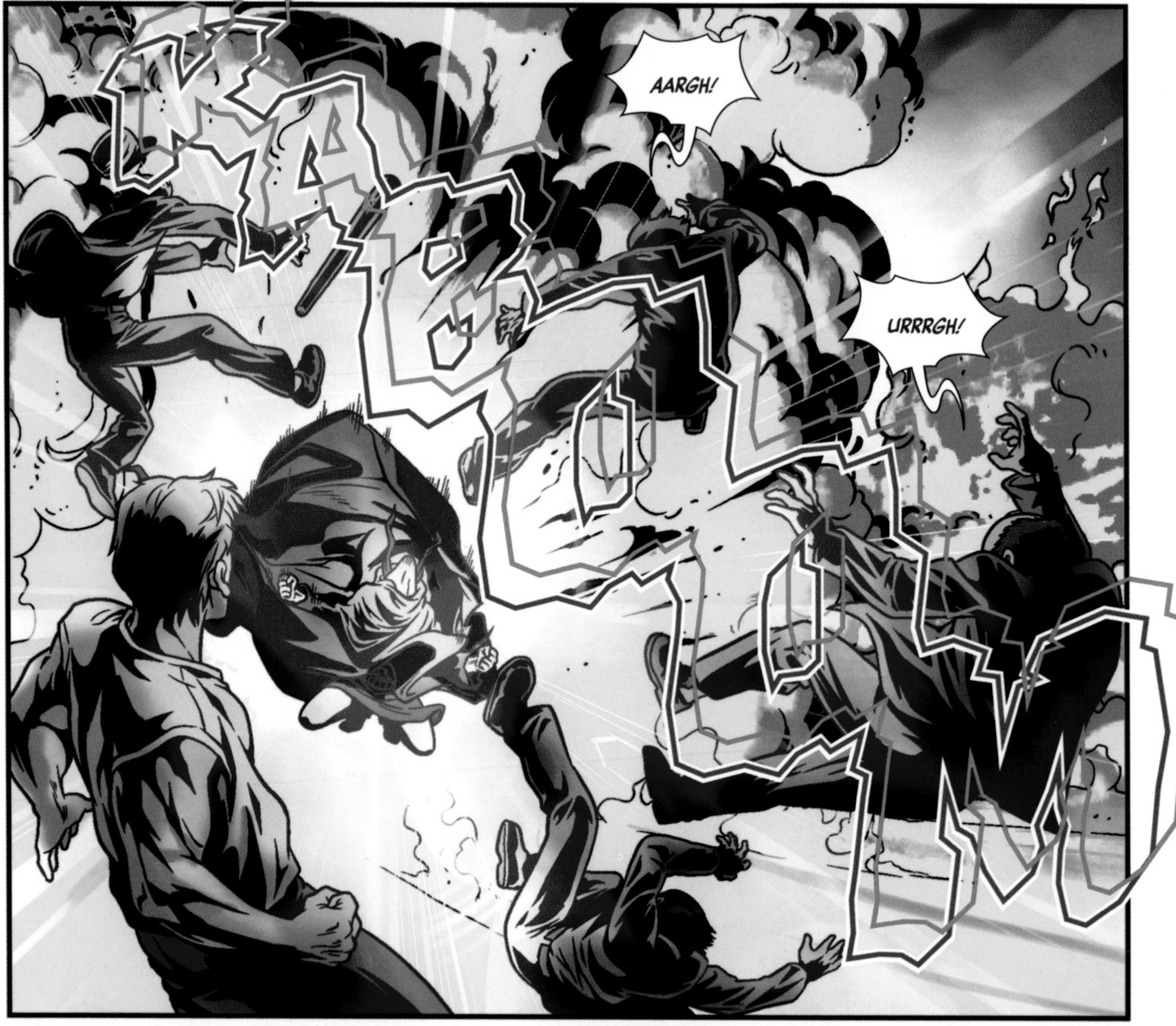
AARGH!
URRRGH!

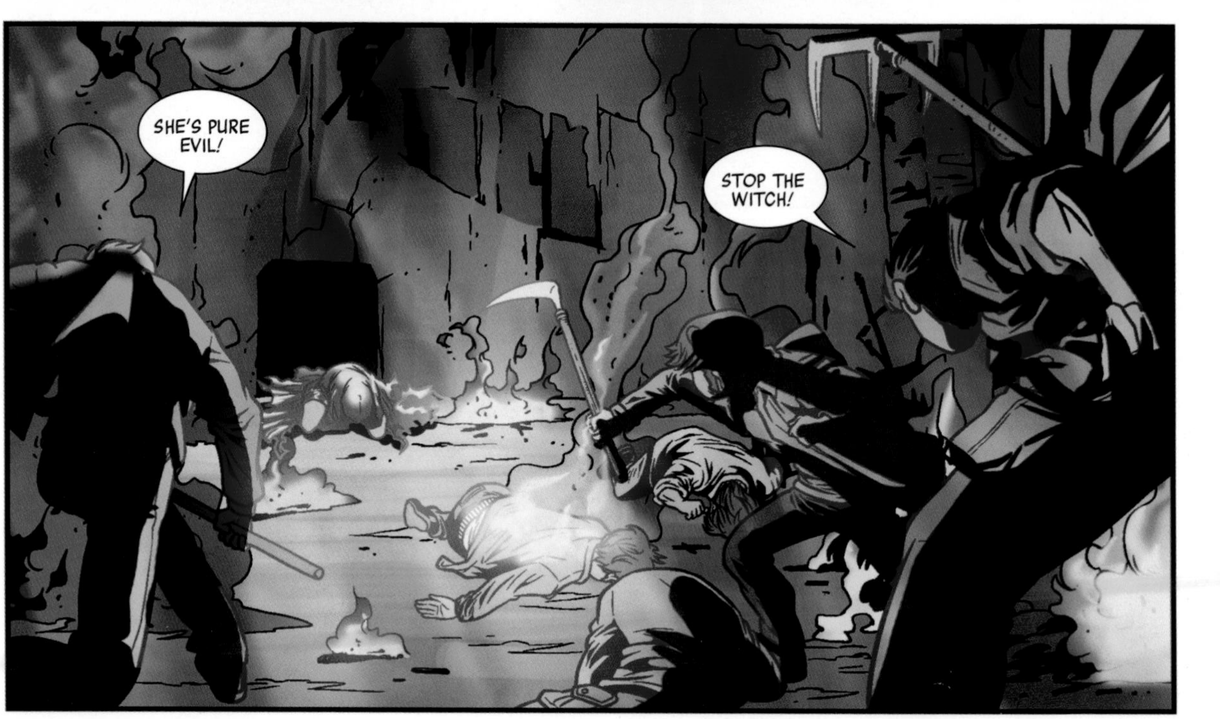
SHE'S PURE EVIL!
STOP THE WITCH!

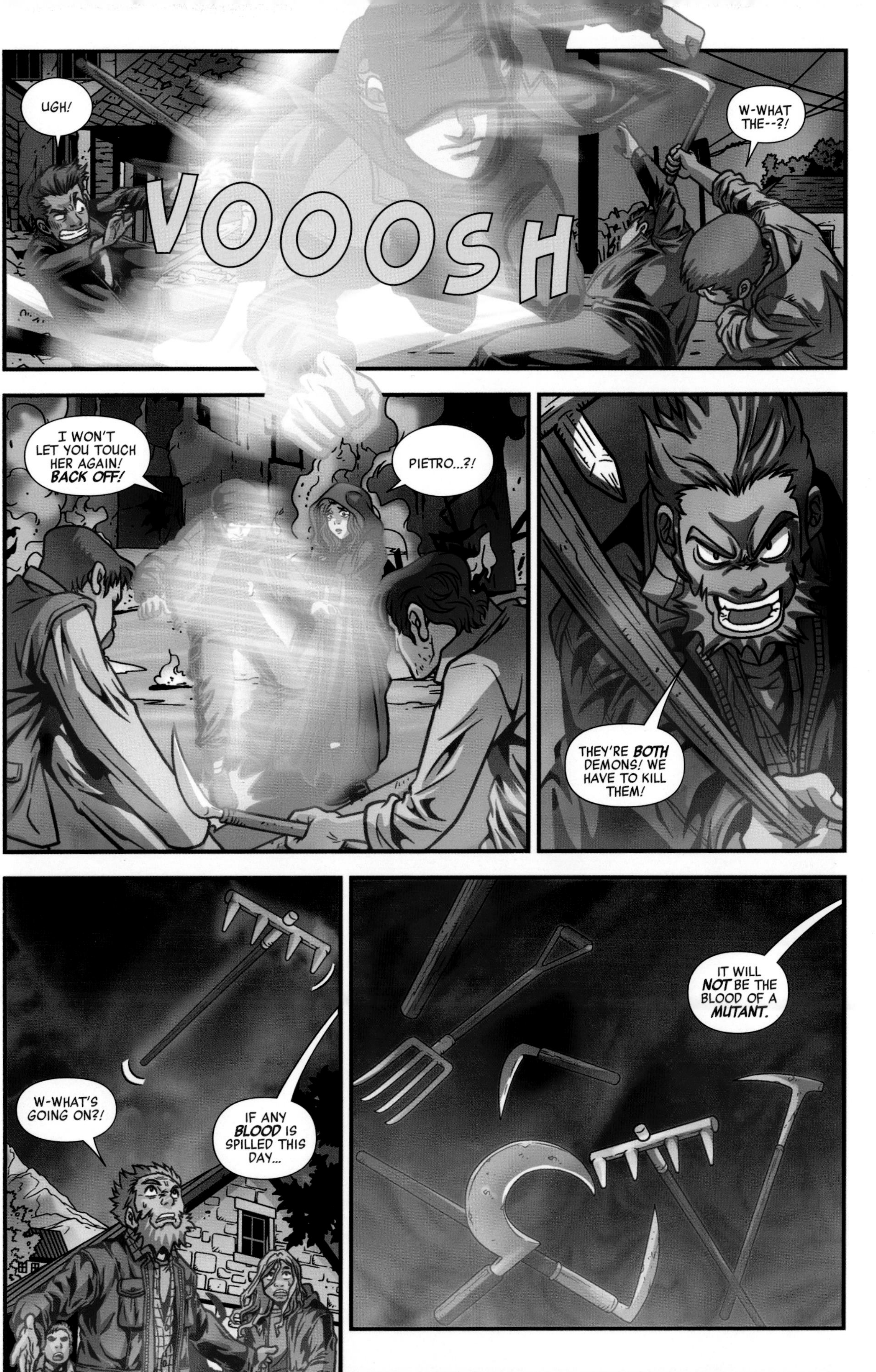
UGH!
VOOOSH
W-WHAT THE--?!
I WON'T LET YOU TOUCH HER AGAIN! BACK OFF!
PIETRO...?!
THEY'RE BOTH DEMONS! WE HAVE TO KILL THEM!
W-WHAT'S GOING ON?!
IF ANY BLOOD IS SPILLED THIS DAY...
IT WILL NOT BE THE BLOOD OF A MUTANT.

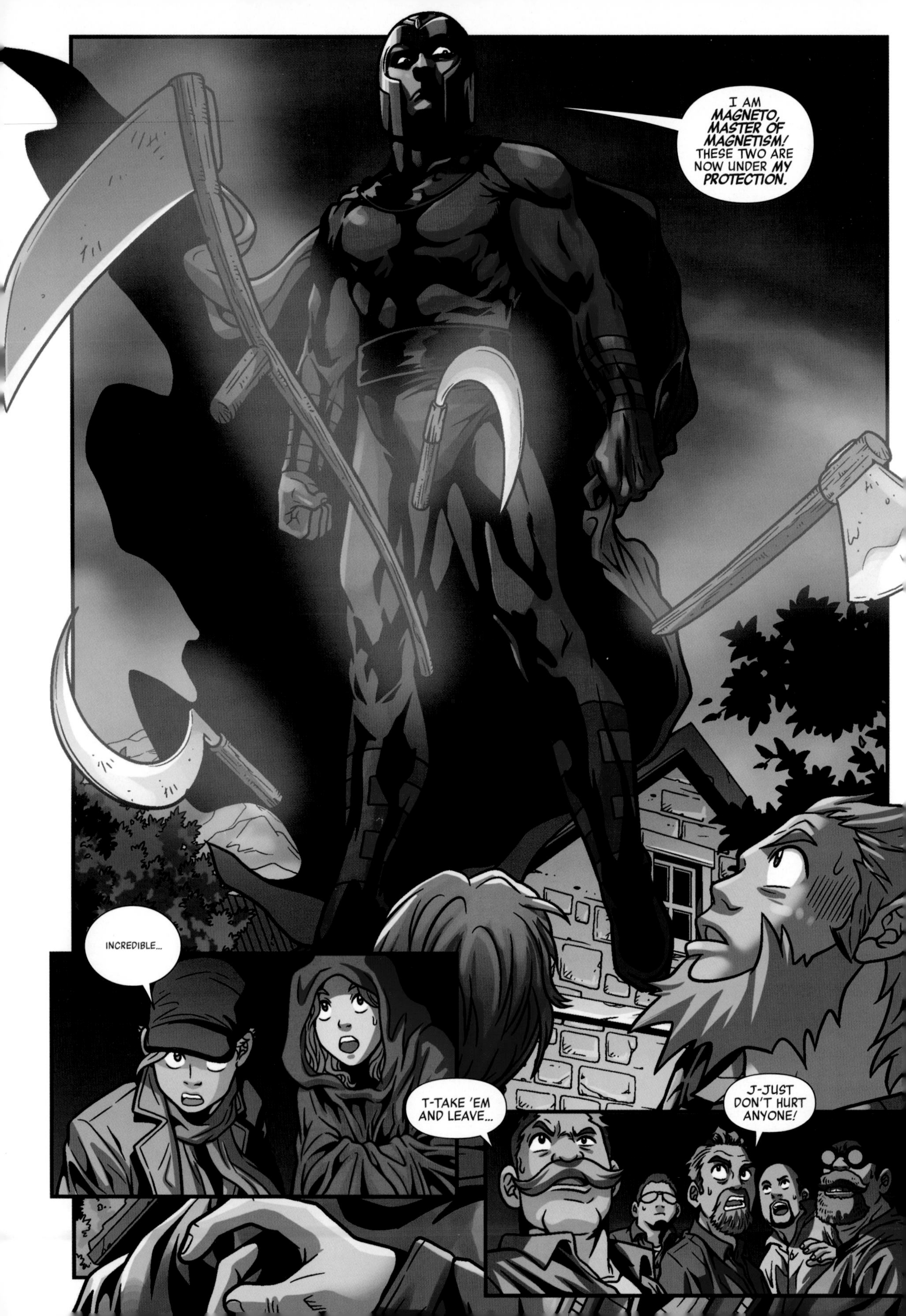

I AM MAGNETO, MASTER OF MAGNETISM! THESE TWO ARE NOW UNDER MY PROTECTION.
INCREDIBLE...
T-TAKE 'EM AND LEAVE...
J-JUST DON'T HURT ANYONE!

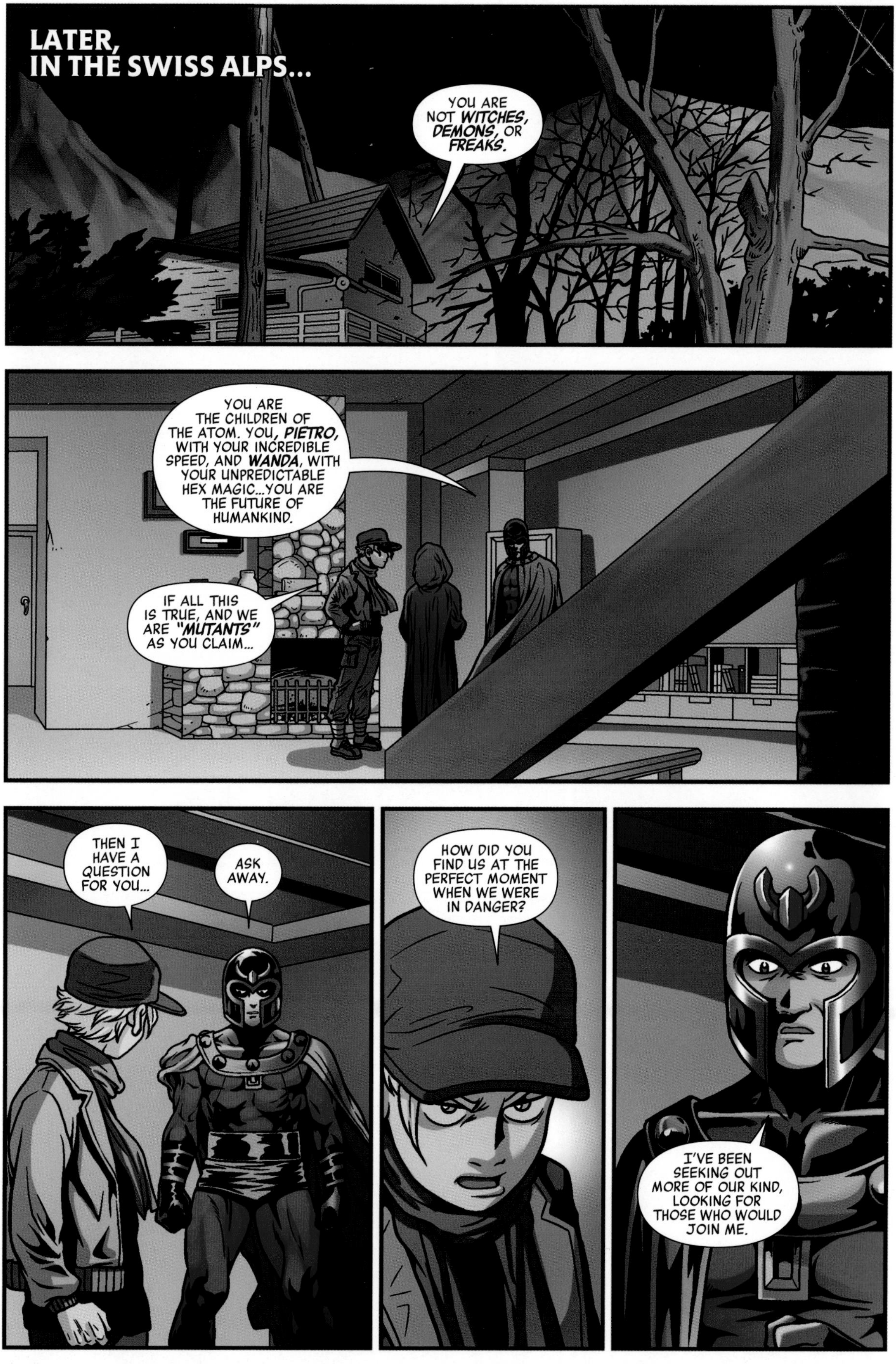
LATER, IN THE SWISS ALPS...
YOU ARE NOT WITCHES, DEMONS, OR FREAKS.
YOU ARE THE CHILDREN OF THE ATOM. YOU, PIETRO, WITH YOUR INCREDIBLE SPEED, AND WANDA, WITH YOUR UNPREDICTABLE HEX MAGIC...YOU ARE THE FUTURE OF HUMANKIND.
IF ALL THIS IS TRUE, AND WE ARE "MUTANTS" AS YOU CLAIM...
THEN I HAVE A QUESTION FOR YOU...
ASK AWAY.
HOW DID YOU FIND US AT THE PERFECT MOMENT WHEN WE WERE IN DANGER?
I'VE BEEN SEEKING OUT MORE OF OUR KIND, LOOKING FOR THOSE WHO WOULD JOIN ME.

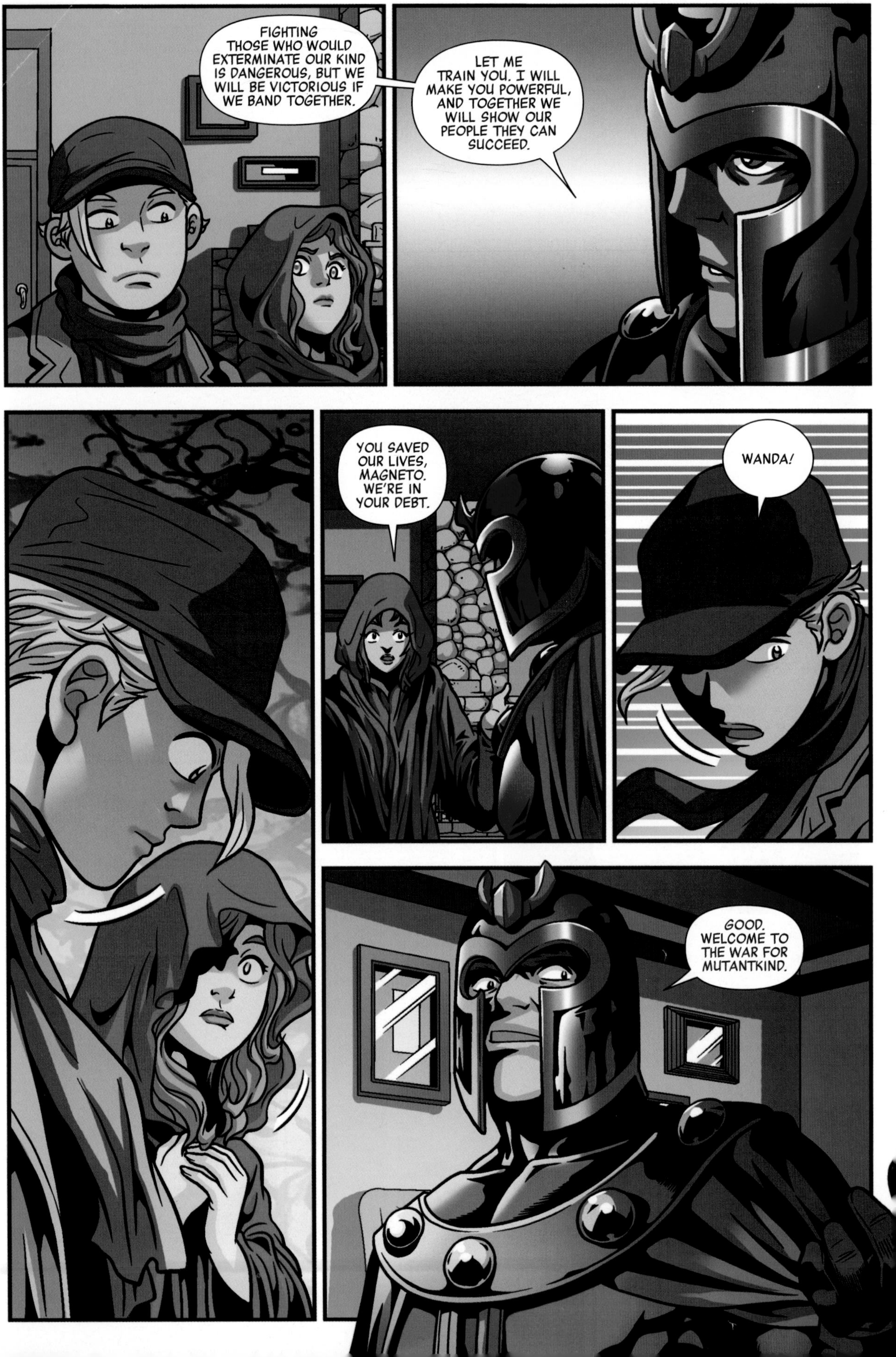
FIGHTING THOSE WHO WOULD EXTERMINATE OUR KIND IS DANGEROUS, BUT WE WILL BE VICTORIOUS IF WE BAND TOGETHER.
LET ME TRAIN YOU. I WILL MAKE YOU POWERFUL, AND TOGETHER WE WILL SHOW OUR PEOPLE THEY CAN SUCCEED.
YOU SAVED OUR LIVES, MAGNETO. WE'RE IN YOUR DEBT.
WANDA!
GOOD. WELCOME TO THE WAR FOR MUTANTKIND.

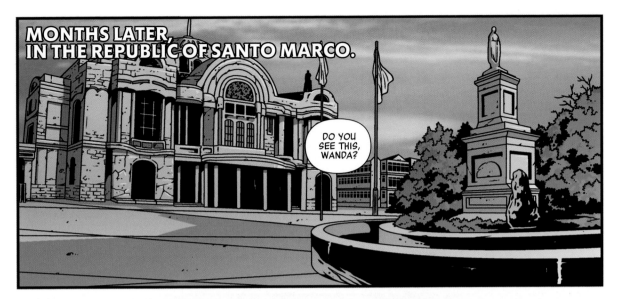

MONTHS LATER,
IN THE REPUBLIC OF SANTO MARCO.

DO YOU SEE THIS, WANDA?

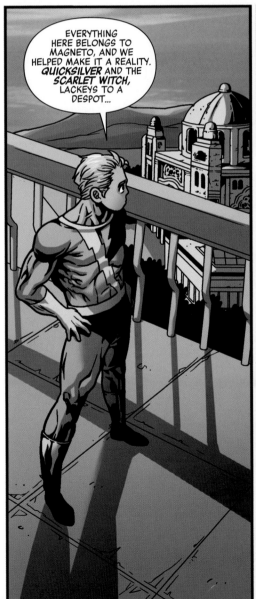

EVERYTHING HERE BELONGS TO MAGNETO, AND WE HELPED MAKE IT A REALITY. *QUICKSILVER* AND THE *SCARLET WITCH*, LACKEYS TO A DESPOT...

WE'RE OVERLORDS. *BULLIES*. PEOPLE ARE AFRAID TO LEAVE THEIR HOMES.

THE GOVERNMENT OF SANTO MARCO WANTED TO KILL ALL MUTANTS.

THEY WERE ALREADY AFRAID OF US.

IF THEY DID COME OUT, IT WOULD ONLY BE TO TRY AND DESTROY US. ERIK--ER, MAGNETO--HAS BEEN GOOD TO US, BROTHER.

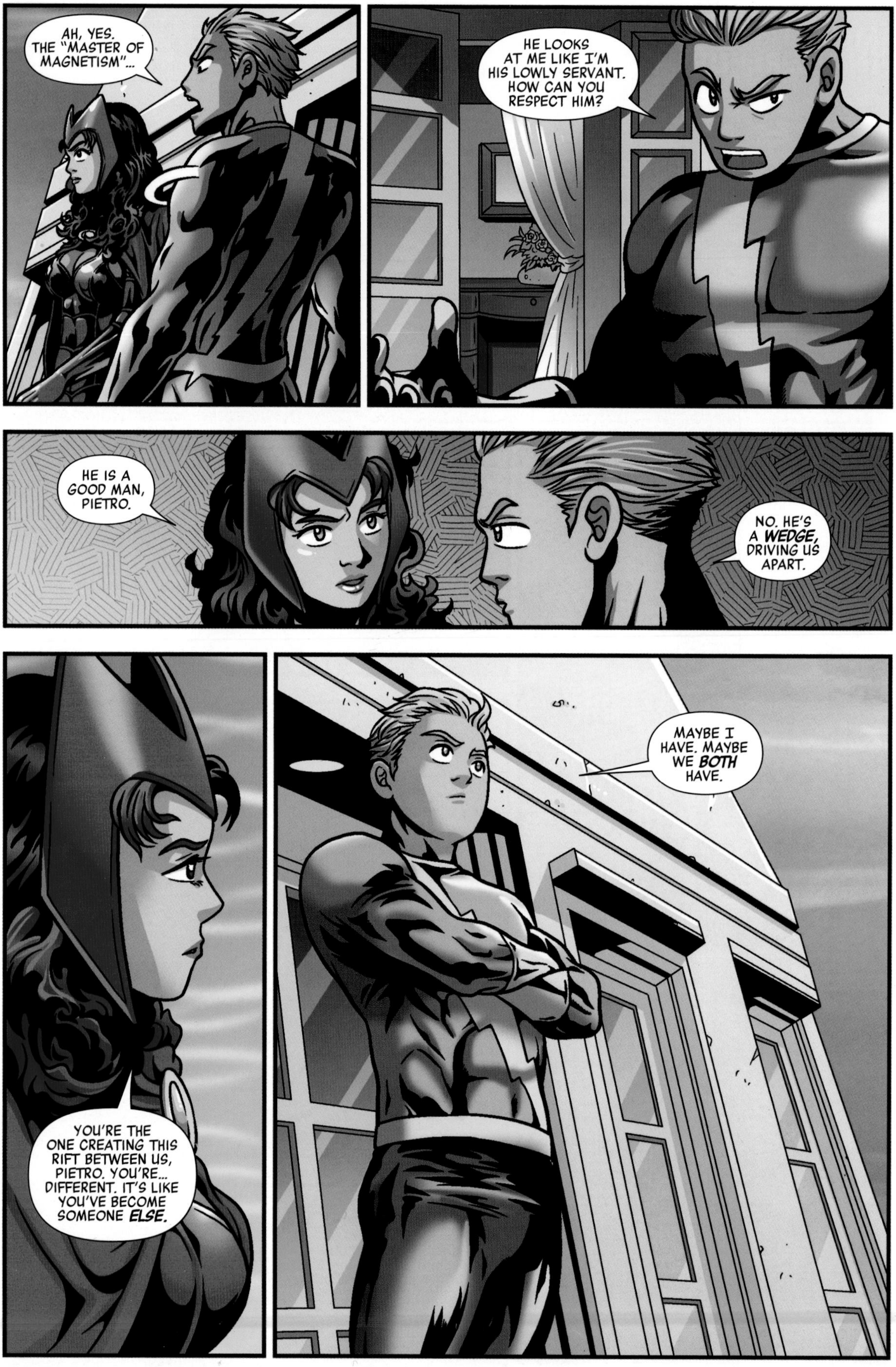
AH, YES. THE "MASTER OF MAGNETISM"...
HE LOOKS AT ME LIKE I'M HIS LOWLY SERVANT. HOW CAN YOU RESPECT HIM?
HE IS A GOOD MAN, PIETRO.
NO. HE'S A **WEDGE**, DRIVING US APART.
YOU'RE THE ONE CREATING THIS RIFT BETWEEN US, PIETRO. YOU'RE... DIFFERENT. IT'S LIKE YOU'VE BECOME SOMEONE **ELSE**.
MAYBE I HAVE. MAYBE WE **BOTH** HAVE.

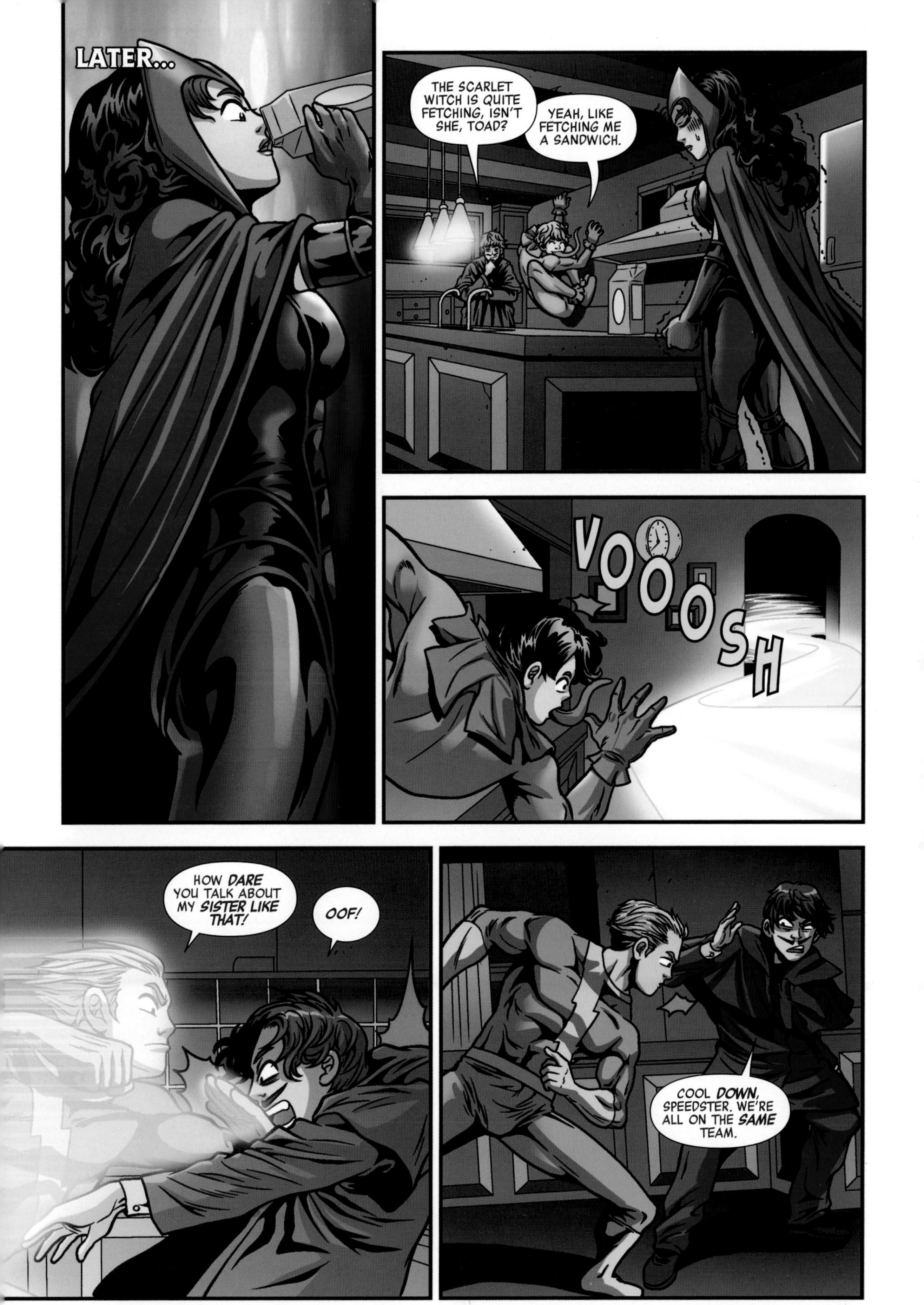
LATER...
THE SCARLET WITCH IS QUITE FETCHING, ISN'T SHE, TOAD?
YEAH, LIKE FETCHING ME A SANDWICH.
VOOOOSH
HOW DARE YOU TALK ABOUT MY SISTER LIKE THAT!
OOF!
COOL DOWN, SPEEDSTER. WE'RE ALL ON THE SAME TEAM.

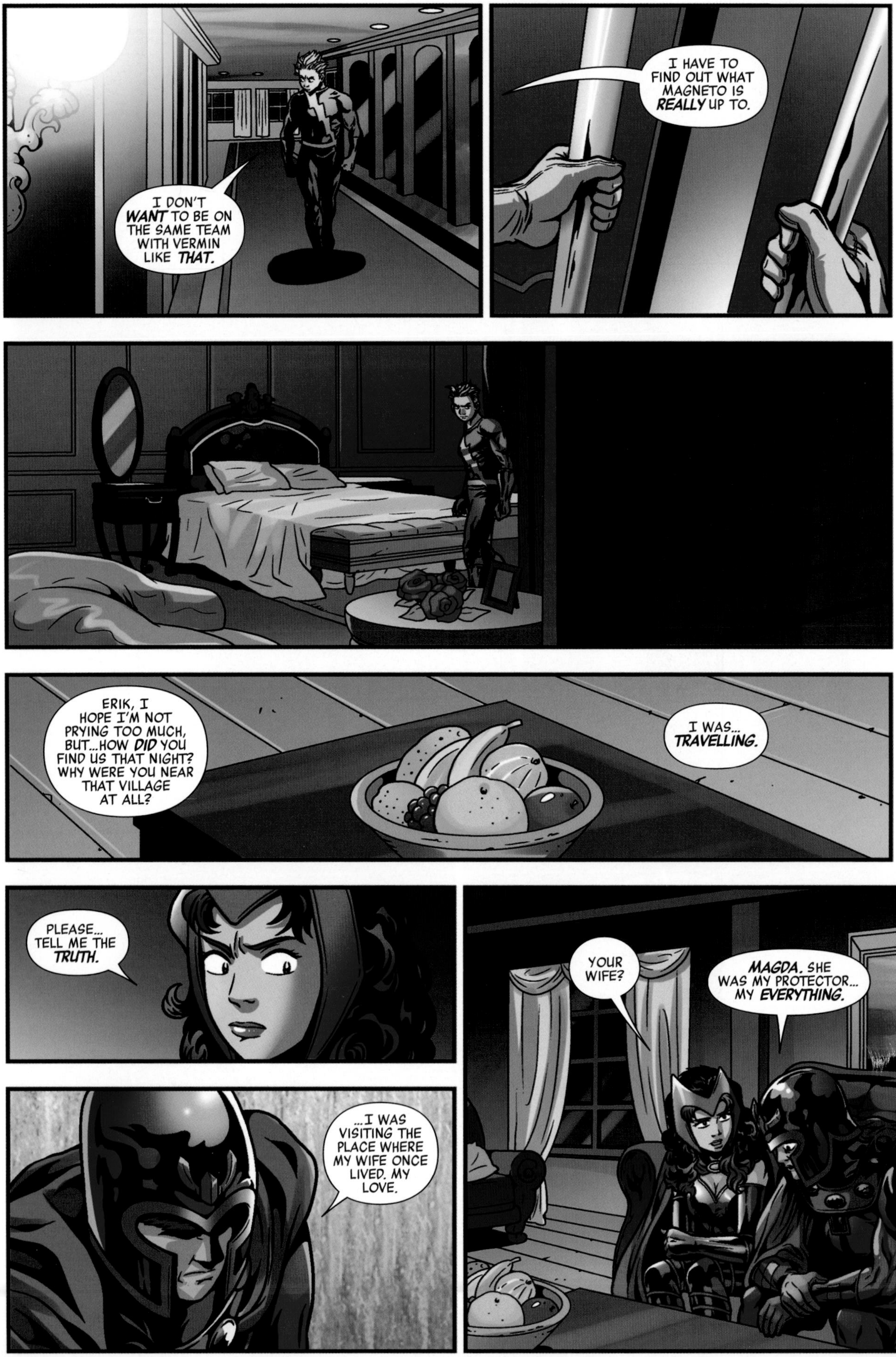
I DON'T WANT TO BE ON THE SAME TEAM WITH VERMIN LIKE THAT.
I HAVE TO FIND OUT WHAT MAGNETO IS REALLY UP TO.
ERIK, I HOPE I'M NOT PRYING TOO MUCH, BUT...HOW DID YOU FIND US THAT NIGHT? WHY WERE YOU NEAR THAT VILLAGE AT ALL?
I WAS... TRAVELLING.
PLEASE... TELL ME THE TRUTH.
...I WAS VISITING THE PLACE WHERE MY WIFE ONCE LIVED. MY LOVE.
YOUR WIFE?
MAGDA. SHE WAS MY PROTECTOR... MY EVERYTHING.

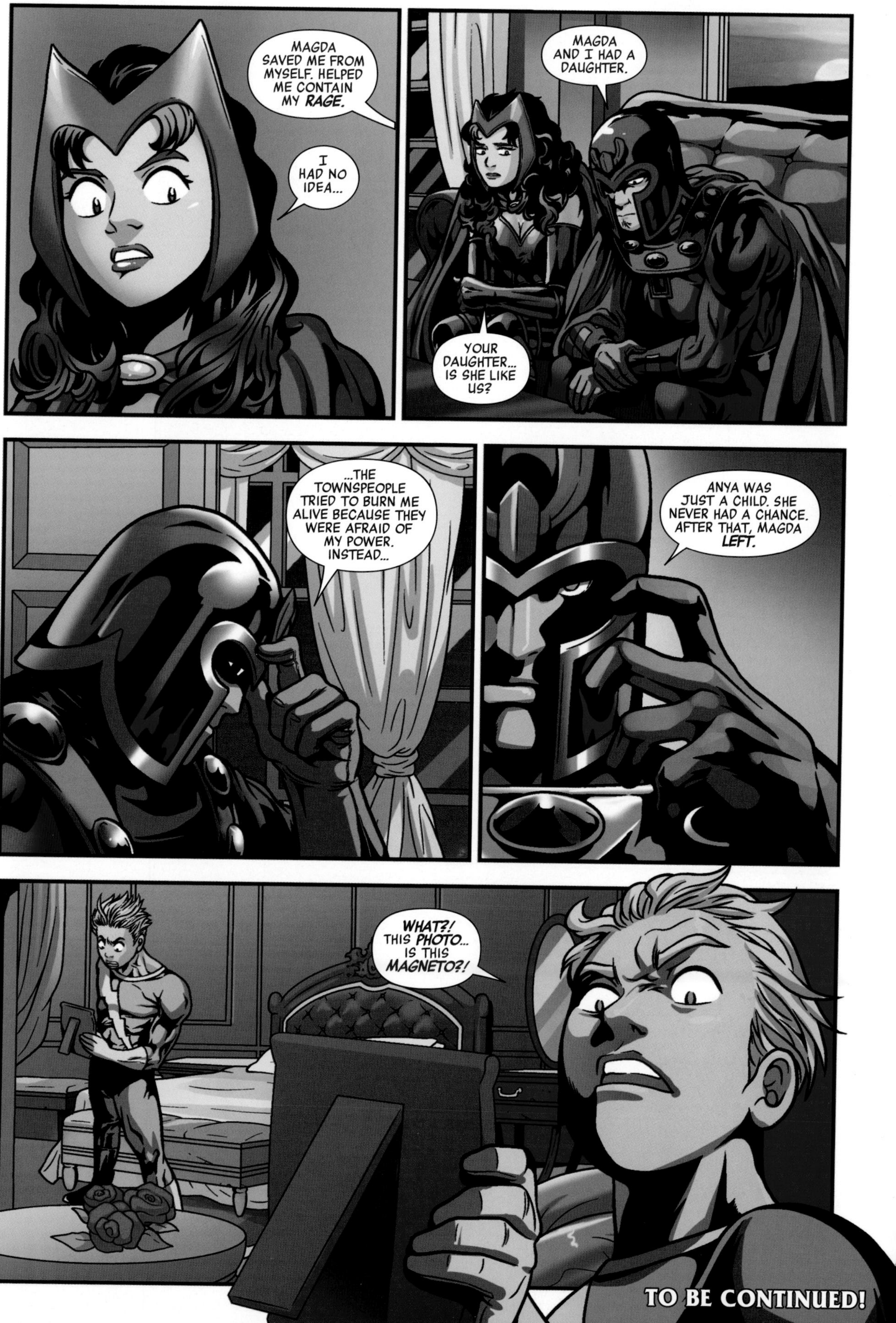

MAGDA SAVED ME FROM MYSELF. HELPED ME CONTAIN MY **RAGE.**
I HAD NO IDEA...
MAGDA AND I HAD A DAUGHTER.
YOUR DAUGHTER... IS SHE LIKE US?
...THE TOWNSPEOPLE TRIED TO BURN ME ALIVE BECAUSE THEY WERE AFRAID OF MY POWER. INSTEAD...
ANYA WAS JUST A CHILD. SHE NEVER HAD A CHANCE. AFTER THAT, MAGDA **LEFT.**
WHAT?! THIS **PHOTO**... IS THIS **MAGNETO?!**
TO BE CONTINUED!

AVENGERS K
THE ADVENT OF ULTRON

COLLECT THEM ALL!
Set of 6 Hardcover Books ISBN: 978-1-5321-4000-6

AVENGERS K
#1
THE ADVENT OF ULTRON
MARVEL

Hardcover Book ISBN
978-1-5321-4001-3

AVENGERS K
#2
THE ADVENT OF ULTRON
MARVEL

Hardcover Book ISBN
978-1-5321-4002-0

AVENGERS K
#3
THE ADVENT OF ULTRON
MARVEL

Hardcover Book ISBN
978-1-5321-4003-7

AVENGERS K
#4
THE ADVENT OF ULTRON
MARVEL

Hardcover Book ISBN
978-1-5321-4004-4

AVENGERS K
#5
THE ADVENT OF ULTRON
MARVEL

Hardcover Book ISBN
978-1-5321-4005-1

AVENGERS K
#6
THE ADVENT OF ULTRON
MARVEL

Hardcover Book ISBN
978-1-5321-4006-8